Harriet's Light

J. H. Bennett

Acknowledgements

My sincere thanks go to Emma Swinden, Emma Carter, Vivienne Harris, Claudia Imms-Harris, Patricia Burton, Viv Burton, Charlie Smith, Ethan Heycock, André Heycock, Craig Kitching, Dan Morris, James Morris and Jake Gomersall.

I would also like to say a big thank you to my wonderful girlfriend Michelle Manion for supporting me whilst I wrote this book.

I am eternally grateful for all of your input and time spent reading this story. You have all helped me bring Harriet to life.

For Harriet, Cyril and my family.

"The night is far spent, the day is at hand:

let us therefore cast off the works of Darkness,

and let us put on the armour of Light"

Romans 13:12

Introduction

Have you ever wondered what a shadow is? The absence of Light? Or something far more sinister? What if I told you that a shadow was not just a place where the Light could not reach and that Light was not just a means of illuminating the Darkness? What if I explained that both Light and Dark were living, feeling entities existing as part of a parallel universe that humans live in completely unaware? Would you believe me? Would you want to? To prove this to you requires an epic story of Light versus Dark, good versus evil. In order to tell it we must cast our minds back to the beginning, the beginning of time to be exact...

At the beginning of time there was only Darkness. Then the Light came, breathing life into the earth, illuminating all that she touched, inching her way across the world and forcing the Darkness to reside only in the deepest of places where Light could never reach.

As time passed the Light and the Darkness became living beings known to us humans as 'Spirits'. Although we are unaware of their presence, these spirits are alive, illuminating and shadowing our world. Without our knowledge they shape our days and our nights and exist all around us.

And so it was for millennia until the Spirit of Darkness grew tired of being dictated to by the Light. Becoming ever greedier for power over the Light's hold he began to force his way out of his deep, shadowy shelter, determined to swallow every inch of Light from the face of the earth and encase the world once more in complete Darkness. The Spirit of Darkness resolutely spread the reach of his shadows into the Light, growing stronger with every spec he consumed until the Spirit of Light became fragile and weak enough to be attacked.

Desperate not to lose her grip on the world, the Spirit of Light turned to the Sorcerers of the present time; an ancient dynasty of conjurors who practised the art of LightCraft; a form of sorcery which used Light Spirit -the very fragments of the Spirit of Light- for assistance. In the hope they would aid her if ever the time should arise, she granted these sorcerers part of herself and her power, which ultimately split the Spirit of Light into separate pieces, as a protection against the Darkness if he should try and consume her.

Together, the sorcerers and the Spirit of Light fought a gruelling battle against the Spirit of Darkness and after much toil were able to abate him enough to be able to control him. To ensure that they could maintain their power over him they locked him away, encased in a shrine of Light and sealed it shut forever.

It was decided that to maintain the balance of Light and Dark, day and night, one of the sorcerers must be offered as a sacrifice and become the new Spirit of Darkness. For many decades the world was at peace. Sorcerers and Spirits lived happily together with the corrupt and evil Darkness safely banished for all eternity.

Or so it would seem...

Chapter 1 - LightCraft

A small village sat upon a hill, home to a colony of Sorcerers who helped the weakened Spirit of Light illuminate the world once more. The shrine they had sealed the Darkness away in had recently began failing and the Darkness was seeping through. The Sorcerers were using all their strength to keep the seal intact, but it was not working. It was only a matter of time before the corrupt Darkness leaked out into their world once more.

These sorcerers lived in very old, stone-walled huts, with thatched roofs made from straw, each of them with a lantern hanging outside the front door. All the fronts of the huts faced the middle of the hill where a giant lantern stood, much like the ones seen around the village. However, this one was huge, it was as tall as the tallest tree in the forest and it looked far more ancient than the others.

Surrounding the village was a dense, dark forest with trees so bent and crooked they looked to be thousands of years old. Some of the trees were so high and vast, that looking up to the top of them made you feel dizzy. On the outskirts of this forest lay ancient lanterns made from a square base of stone which grew upwards with a curve into a small point supporting the hollow glass orb on top that houses the Light. This allows for maximum illumination from all angles. The stone at the bases of the lanterns were engraved in a language understood by only a few humans -the language of the Light. These lanterns formed a loop around the entire outskirts of the forest like a fence and met at the forest entrance, where a single, long-winding pathway -with lanterns laid on both sides of the path- ran all the way up to the top of the hill. At the top of the pathway the lanterns branched out and looped around the entire hill surrounding the village.

In one of these little huts lived a young girl named Harriet. Harriet was a sweet little girl who was very shy and always wore the hood of her robe -a light beige coloured robe that she made herself, with a piece of rope tied around her waist as a belt- up to conceal herself. She saw her hood as a source of protection and comfort but her mother was always telling her to take it off to show her cute, pretty face. Harriet had luscious dark brown, almost black, slightly wavy hair with subtle hints of white that could only be seen when struck by light. Harriet's life consisted of helping her mother with cooking, cleaning, making clothes, helping the villagers with anything that needed doing and her most important and favourite thing was practising LightCraft; a form of sorcery where fragments of the Spirit of Light were called upon for assistance. Her mother, father and all the people she knew were sorcerers that specialised in LightCraft. She had been around magic since she was born and even at a very young age Harriet was extremely adept at LightCraft -better than all the other children in the village and most of the adults too. However, even with her great powers she was still a shy little girl who was terrified of the Dark.

It was late morning and Harriet was walking along the winding pathway down the hill from the village, to where all the children were in the field below attending LightCraft school -a school that teaches the children about the techniques of summoning Light Spirit to use defensively and offensively against the Darkness. These lessons were held every day and were taught by Harriet's mother, Vespera; an old but extremely powerful sorceress who had lived in the village since it was originally built. She gave birth to Harriet a few months after the Darkness was defeated and sealed away and is looked up to by everyone as their leader and guide. Vespera was tall and elegant with thick, long, grey, almost white hair that flowed through the air like seaweed in water. She wore a long, beige robe that was extremely old and heavy but still in good condition for its age, except for a few frayed edges on her sleeves. Draped around her neck was a long dark brown scarf that fell down both sides of her neck. On both ends of this scarf were identical symbols; a white outline of a triangle with three circles on both sides of it, with one circle above the top point. The wooden staff she carried around with her looked like it was older than she was; it bared the same markings as the lanterns, but they seemed to be losing themselves in the wood from the many years of use. On top of the staff was an orb that housed Light Spirit and looked extremely powerful, an incredible sight to behold for anyone lucky enough to see it up close. Vespera had an air of confidence about her which had stemmed from being the head of the village for so many generations.

Her father, Alucio; a strong, old sorcerer who was also directly involved with the capture of the Darkness, wore a long dark beige coloured robe with a few large tears in it. He refused to make a new one as it served as a reminder of the monumental battle and capture of the Darkness. He had long, grey hair and a mid length, fuzzy, grey beard; both of which had subtle hints of a very dark brown -almost black- in. Alucio loved Harriet more than anything and, much to the dismay of her mother, was always teaching her LightCraft that the younger children are not allowed to perform. He always carried his staff around with him which also showed marks of damage from the battle; the wood of the staff had scratches on it like it had been clawed into, and the glass orb atop the staff was cracking with some small, hairline fractures. Along with Vespera, he was also in charge of the village. His duties included maintaining anything that needed doing in the village, and leading the hunting pack for food in the forest with the other males who lived there.

The sun was shining down from a clear blue sky, casting its rays on a mist still lingering above the lake from the cold of the night. A slight, but pleasantly cool breeze was blowing its way through the field, gently pushing the mist into the forest, making it look haunted. Harriet was nearly at the base of the hill now and she could see the children looking at her with sly glances, muttering to themselves. Harriet was not very popular among the children and they took a dislike to her because of the power she possessed. However, she always tried her best to rise above them, and as usual, she just walked right past the children, paying them no attention. They sometimes upset her but she did not want them knowing it got to her.

Her mother called to her from across the field.

"Harriet darling, over here please."

Harriet walked over to her mother.

"Good morning my dear, how are you today?" her mother said to her.

"I am OK thank you Mother," she said with a huge yawn, "Sorry for being late I did not get much

16

sleep again last night," she stretched her arms out and yawned again.

"That is quite alright my love, class has not started yet anyway. Your father wanted to speak to you before we begin. Would you go and see him please, he is over by the tree at the lake."

"OK mother, I shall go and see him now," said Harriet and she walked over to her father, pondering what he wanted to speak to her about.

The tree where he was standing was so close to the lake that the big roots of it were squirming through the mud and into the water. Fish were nestling among the entanglement of roots, peeking out of their hiding spots with their eyes glistening in the sun.

She approached her father who was stood looking out across the lake into the forest.

"Hello father, you wanted to see me?" said Harriet.

"Well hello little one. How are you this morning? Are you ready for the trials today?" his voice was deep and weathered with a slight croak to it.

"Yes I am, although I am feeling really sleepy today," she replied.

"You should not stay up so late practising LightCraft, it will wear you out."

"I cannot sleep in the Dark, it scares me father."

"Harriet, do not be silly, there is nothing to be afraid of now, but more importantly I wanted to talk to you about the trials. You do know that you do not have to take the trials, you are already good enough."

"No father I must. I get enough grief off the other children as it is, I do not wish to give them any more reasons to pick on me, plus I want to take the exam, as a test to myself," she said assertively.

"I do not want you getting involved in something that could give you pain Harriet."

"What do you mean? I will be perfectly alright, I have gotten along just fine ignoring them anyway."

"Very well... then you must do your best little one, as we will be assessing you strictly like the others. There is no leniency just because you are our daughter."

"Of course Father, I expect nothing less. I will give it my best and I will not let you down."

Alucio smiled and gave her a hug and whispered into her ear "Be strong little one, I will always love you no matter what."

Harriet looked confused as to why he would say this.

"I... love you too father," they let go of each other and headed back to the rest of the group. As they walked back to the group he had his hand rested on her shoulder.

"Make me proud Harriet," he tapped her on her back and walked over to stand next to Vespera.

All the children were sat down on the grass by the lake looking towards Harriet's mother and father. Harriet joined the children, sitting at the front, away from them all. They all faced her mother who was about to address the class.

"Good Morning everyone," said Vespera.

"Good morning Miss," the children replied.

"I hope you all had a decent night's sleep, as today is the big day for you all," said Alucio.

The children began to fidget excitedly.

"Today is the day that we assess your LightCraft skills. If you can complete the trials we ask of you then you will become a Protector of Light. Firstly we would like you all to stand up and line side by side with your backs to the lake," said Vespera.

All the children stood up and began to make a line. Some chose to stand by certain friends and were swapping their positions around. Eventually they had positioned themselves in a line standing side by side.

Harriet was stood on her own at the end of the line next to a girl called Kira who seemed to pay her a curious amount of attention, unlike the other horrible children.

Vespera and Alucio were discussing something whilst the children watched on in an anxious gaze.

"I am so excited!" said one of the children.

"Me too! I have been practising day and night for this."

"Harriet," Kira said to her awkwardly, half expecting to get a blank response.

"Yes?" replied Harriet.

"Would you...like to pair up with me today?" Harriet felt shocked, no one had ever asked her to pair up, or play, or be friends, and she felt slightly embarrassed.

"OK... will not you get teased by the other children for speaking and pairing with me though?"

"Ah I do not care what they think," said Kira, "I think your powers are amazing."

This made Harriet blush. It was the first time in her life that she experienced anything in the form of a friendship.

"Thank you, Kira? Is it not?"

"Yeah that is me," she said with a huge teeth-baring smile.

"Thank you..." Harriet did not know why, but she felt all warm and fuzzy inside.

"OK everyone. Firstly we would like to see you recite the Elder's Tribute," said Vespera.

This made the children become awkward and embarrassed, chatting amongst themselves saying, "I do not want to do it," whilst others said, "I do not know it."

"Settle down, settle down. Harriet, would you please kindly do the honour of reminding everyone why we take these trials of Light."

Harriet stepped forward and stood in front of her mother and father, turning around to face the class who were all gazing straight at her -she did not like this feeling of being stared at and felt a surge of nervousness running through her, making her blush. Before she began she shut her eyes and took a couple of deep breaths to relax and she tried to imagine the children were not there.

"These trials of Light are a tribute to the Elders that fought to give us back the Light when the Darkness almost won. Their strength and determination gave us the lives that we cherish today. To commemorate their fearless bravery, we show our honour and appreciation by demonstrating that we too, can ward off the Darkness."

Harriet finished and sat back down among the children.

"Thank you Harriet, that was lovely," said her mother, "I hope all of you understand this completely. These trials are to be taken seriously."

"Now it is time to start the trial. Firstly we would like to see you produce a standard Lēoht -Lēoht is a word meaning Illuminate, stemming from the sorcerers long before them- I know this is not anything advanced, but it is a crucial and fundamental part of LightCraft. We want you to maintain your Lēoht until we have assessed your control of the Light Spirit," said Alucio.

The children began summoning their Lēoht, most of them Lighting up instantly. A few children were struggling to summon any Light Spirit at all and were becoming restless.

"Agh, why can I not summon it?" a girl screamed.

"Focus your thoughts. Do not let the pressure hinder your mind, relaxation is the key," Vespera said to her.

"Sorry Miss, I do not know what came over me," she paused for a few seconds and shut her eyes, taking a few deep breaths and said "Lēoht!" making her palms instantly fill with Light Spirit. Vespera smiled and gently nodded to her in appreciation.

Harriet's parents were walking up and down the line of children, assessing each of the children's Lēoht as they passed. Harriet produced a perfectly steady and illuminated Light and her parents nodded at her in approval. One child, who was standing only a couple of children away from Harriet, was straining hard, trying to maintain his Lēoht as it began to flicker on and off erratically. He was only seven and he was the youngest in the class, only five years younger than Harriet.

"Be calm, do not force the Light child," Vespera said to the young boy, "The more stress you put into summoning the Light, the less it will want to come to you, you have to relax."

"Yes... Miss," he said nervously.

"Now, take a deep breath, calm yourself down and try again."

The other children were now watching him out the corner of their eyes, totally unfocused on their own Lēoht flickering out. The boy took a deep breath.

Focussing intensely on the empty space between his hands he cast Lēoht again; Light began to appear in the air all around his hands, flowing towards his palms, some of the Light was passing through his hands Lighting them up red. It gathered and swirled around to create a solid ball of Light with tiny specs of Light Spirit swirling around on the inside of it, casting off a brilliant bright blue -almost white- glow, illuminating his hands and face. As the boy stood there, casting the best Lēoht he had ever cast, everyone cheered for him. He was so focused on his Lēoht that this startled him. He lost focus and his light faded. He looked around at everyone clapping and cheering.

Vespera smiled proudly.

"Well done child."

He let a big smile fill his face. Feeling happy and embarrassed from all the attention, he shied away, twiddling his thumbs bashfully.

"Well done, you managed to keep your calm and summon Lēoht. You have proven yourself and have passed this first trial, you should be proud!"

"Thank you Miss."

"The rest of you have passed too, but do not get too excited yet, we have two more trials to go. The next trial will examine your ability to attack using Light Spirit," Alucio said as he produced objects made of Light for each of the children. The objects looked like glittering crystal statues that were glowing intensely, standing out, even in the afternoon Light.

"OK. I shall now explain this trial to you. These statues will diminish when struck by Light Spirit, but they regenerate after a certain time so you need to attack the target methodically and tactfully. I will not divulge ways you can achieve your goal, that is for each of you to work out for yourself."

The children were really lively now, some of them getting a bit too eager as their hands were already alight with Light Spirit -like a pair of electric gloves-shooting off sparks of Light.

"We will do this one at a time as we need to assess you individually as you all have different skills and techniques," as Alucio said this, a stream of Light shot out of his hand creating a line of Light on the ground. The children lined up behind it anxiously.

"Good luck Harriet. I cannot wait for you to see what I can do," said Kira.

"Thanks, I look forward to seeing it too."

The child at the other end of the line was the first to go, so Kira and Harriet would be the last ones.

"All of you take heed of this! Focus only on the statue ahead of you, imagine it is an enemy and your very life depends on it, because a real enemy will not let you attack it without a fight!" said Vespera.

"Yes, yes that is quite right. Are you ready child? On my mark you shall begin." Alucio said.

The child faced the statue and posed ready with his right leg back, hands at shoulder height and palms facing forwards. Eagerness and excitement was flowing through him. His hands lit up with Light as he waited to start. He clenched his fists, compressing the Darkness Spirit from his hands into balls.

"Ready... Begin!" Vespera shouted.

At that moment, balls of Light were sent hurtling through the field colliding with the Light statue, sending sparks of Light exploding off in all directions. The children were shouting and cheering him on making quite a racket on the field. This had attracted some attention from the village above as they could hear distant words of encouragement being shouted. Vespera was standing behind the child checking his stance and technique whilst Alucio was standing in the field near to the statues watching how effective their LightCraft was at attacking.

The boy continued to fling Light at the statue, clenching his fists and opening them as he threw his Light forward -it seemed as if he was throwing an infinite number of bright white tennis balls from his hands. He had almost destroyed the statue, but the final part of it kept regenerating and rebuilding itself upwards. Alucio was watching the boy intently to see how he was going to tackle the situation. He clenched his fists together and closed his eyes, his face was as calm as a still ocean. His fists were intensifying with Light Spirit at a dramatic rate and his hands were shaking making his arms rattle. He opened his eyes, and calmly looked at his target. His hands were so bright and the glow was so big that no one could see his face.

He shouted, "Warghhh," throwing both hands forward letting loose a huge cluster of Light balls from each hand. The balls flew through the air all at once and the other children stood watching, totally amazed.

The constant battering of multiple balls of Light forced the Light statue down until it extinguished.

Vespera approached him.

"Excellent skills child, you have passed. You may sit down and rest now."

"Thank you Miss," he said and he turned around and went to sit by the lake, being praised by the children as he walked over.

Harriet was amazed at this child's ability to create multiple balls of Light like that at such a young age. She felt very proud of him.

The children all faced off against their statues, some of them passed whilst others failed. It was now Kira's turn. Harriet stepped back to give her some space.

"Watch this," Kira said to Harriet.

"Begin!" shouted Vespera.

Kira tested out the regeneration by throwing some basic Light balls at the statue, like she was testing for weaknesses. So far it was not impressive and Harriet felt a bit awkward for her. After shooting its arms off and seeing how they grew back, she stopped and summoned Lēoht once more. She rubbed her palms together in a circular motion like she was rolling a ball of dough. Gradually in small circles, growing into bigger ones until her hands were just moving around in the air. She had made a disc of Light. Kira took hold of it and threw it, carving through the air straight at the statue, slicing off its limbs -like a knife through butter- before it curved around and returned back to her hands. Harriet was stunned. She did not imagine that Kira was so good at LightCraft. She continued throwing the disc at it, slicing it to pieces until it was no more.

"Well done Kira that was fantastic! You have got exceptional LightCraft skills," said Vespera.

"Thank you Miss, thank you very much," she was thrilled.

"What do you think Harriet? I have been working on that for a while now."

"That was just, amazing. I never knew you were that good!"

"Thank you, that means a lot. Now it is my turn to see what you do, I cannot wait!"

"Alright," said Harriet as she began to walk towards the line of Light, feeling uncomfortable being in the spotlight under everyone's eyes. She could hear the children sniggering and making fun of her. But she ignored it.

Harriet turned to face her statue, readying herself confidently although she was terrified inside as she was now under the watch of the entire village. The rest of the children had finished and were sat by the lake. The villagers were now down in the field and were stood with her parents who were watching her too. She gained her resolve, thinking only about defeating the statue. She blocked out everything and everyone else with such an intense focus, it was as if there was not a soul around her, just herself and the statue of Light. She took a few deep breaths and summoned her Lēoht; her hands were beaming with more Light than all the other children's Lēoht combined, filling the afternoon air around her with Light Spirit. She built up her Lēoht so big that she disappeared among the huge Light cast from her hands. Her hands poked out either side and the Light began shrinking -she was compressing the Light into a more compact ball, amplifying its power. Her arms came down to her sides and her hands came together in front of her with the compressed ball of Light between them, which was now the size of a large pumpkin. Harriet raised her elbows up and outwards, turning her palms to face forward, and like a swimmer performing a breast stroke, she tore apart the powerful ball of Light as if it was nothing, sending it flying off to her sides. The balls of Light soared outwards through the air, curving in and colliding with each other, combining to make one huge sphere of Light hovering just a few metres above the statue.

There was so much compression you could see the Light Spirit squashed together trying to escape like an over filled balloon. Everyone was now fixated on Harriet. She summoned up Lēoht again and as she clasped her palms together her hands were shrouded in an intense Light. She raised her arms above her head and brought them down in a slicing motion, firing a Light spear directly towards the ball of Light. The spear pierced into the ball, setting off a huge explosion creating strands of Light that shot downwards penetrating through the statue like a thousand swords. Each of the strands then exploded, totally obliterating the statue.

"Whoa! Amazing! " shouted Kira, "That was incredible Harriet."

"... Thanks," Harriet did not think that what she had done was that impressive. It was all second nature to her.

"Well, I guess it is safe to say you have passed the trial my dear," said Vespera, "You have really improved your LightCraft skills Harriet."

"Thank you Mother, I tried my best," said Harriet.

A couple of children that didn't like Harriet scoffed and turned their noses up at her in disgust.

"Heh, what a show off," said one girl, "of course she passed, the teachers are her parents!"

Harriet ignored them and walked away to sit by the lake. She sat by the water's edge with her knees up, her arms wrapped around them resting her face on her knees. Kira came and sat next to her.

"Forget them Harriet do not give them the time of day, just petty jealousy is what it is. What you just did was astonishing. I wish I could do that, and so do they."

"I do not care for them, it does not bother me anymore. Thanks for your concern though, nobody else cares for my feelings."

"Of course, we are friends are we not?"

Harriet felt embarrassed again.

"I guess so? I have never had a friend before."

"It is settled then, we are friends!" giggled Kira.

They both grinned and laughed. Harriet never laughed and her mother and father saw these two new friends and smiled.

"It is about time she found a friend," Alucio said.

"I know, I am so happy for her. She has needed one for so long now," replied Vespera.

Harriet and Kira turned to face the lake behind them which was catching the reflections of their LightCraft remnants dancing in the sky.

"I love this, just sitting here watching the Light. It makes me forget."

"What do you need to forget?" asked Kira.

"Oh… nothing, forget I said anything."

"No, we are friends now. We tell each other things like this. Come on what is it?"

"It is..." Harriet paused, "I just I feel so alone. Apart from my mother and father the only thing I have is my Light Spirit to keep me company."

"I am so sorry Harriet that must have been awful all of this time. I am sorry I did not talk to you before, it was nothing personal. The other children made up stories about you to scare each other from talking to you."

"Oh how lovely..." Harriet muttered sarcastically.

"It is OK you have got me now and you are not getting out of it! Have you played with someone else's light before?"

"No I have not. What does that involve?" Harriet asked her curiously.

"Summon your Light and you will see, well you will 'feel'. It is like you are holding someone else's hand and moving it about. It is hard to explain unless you experience it. You will see."

Harriet and Kira turned facing each other and summoned up their Light Spirit. They were sat for a short while playing with their Lēoht together, creating intertwining Light between their hands. Their Lights were wrapping around each other's like tree roots growing, making a beautiful entanglement. Harriet's Light was an intense white, whereas Kira's was a brilliantly bright pale blue with sparks of white.

"It feels like I am touching your hand," Harriet said.

"I told you. You cannot explain this feeling, you have to try it."

They heard Vespera and Alucio approaching and stopped playing. They both pulled their hands away, making their Light break apart and shatter in mid-air creating a spectacle of pale blue and white sparks against the late afternoon sky.

"Everyone, please gather round we have an announcement to make," Alucio said. All the children got up and stood near to them to hear what they had to say.

"Well done to all of you, we are very impressed with your abilities so far and all of you have passed the first trial of Light," Vespera said to the children.

The children jumped for joy, cheering.

"Yessss!" "Wahoooo!"

"The final trial will take place this evening when the sun has gone down, so all of you must meet us at the village lantern after I have performed the daily Lighting. I shall explain the details of the next trial there, so until then you are free to play and enjoy the afternoon."

"Well done everyone, you are all very talented. I am most impressed with your efforts today," Alucio said to them before he and Vespera left to return to the village.

"Yay we did it! Let us go home and have some tea until the trial tonight Harriet," Kira said.

"I am going to stay down here on my own for a bit if you do not mind," replied Harriet.

"OK if you are sure, I shall see you this evening then. Take care," she skipped off through the field bursting with happiness.

Harriet had climbed the tree by the lake and was sat alone with her legs dangling over a branch, swaying them backwards and forwards gently in the air. The tree was next to the small lake that they were sat by; it ran from a stream in the forest and into the lake behind her. She would sit here on her own practising her spells after LightCraft School every day. The children who were still in the field were playing a game with their LightCraft similar to tennis, which required the summoning of a Light barrier instead of a racquet. The players had to summon Light just at the right time in order to conjure up a barrier of Light to deflect the ball of Light back, or else it would hit that person with a small jolt and they would be out of the game. Harriet watched briefly from time to time from the tree, but she was more focused on her LightCraft. As she was sitting in the tree she could hear the children chuckling and making fun of her. One child was calling her a "freak," and another was saying "She thinks she's so special," but Harriet was used to it now and just brushed it off as if she couldn't even hear them.

As the sun started to set, fireflies began to emerge in the field all around the children. They tried playing with them by using their LightCraft to attract them, but the fireflies seemed uninterested and only seemed to be attracted to Harriet. They all flew to her and surrounded her, Lighting the tree up like a Christmas tree - enveloping it in a vibrant pale pink glow. The children got bored of trying to play with the fireflies and decided to go back to the village. Harriet heard one of them say.

"Look at her the freak, those fireflies are her only friends hahaha."

The children all started laughing and walked off towards their homes. Harriet ignored it. She put her hands out, cupped them together and a single firefly flew into the space between her hands and hovered there as if it was enjoying the comfort of her presence. The other fireflies close to her hands were dancing about as if they were jealous of that firefly. Harriet gazed at it intently for a while, just staring at it forgetting about everything around her until it flew away.

She climbed down from the tree, still surrounded by countless fireflies and began to head home. Still being followed and completely shrouded by the fireflies, she began to twirl and dance whilst walking through the field as if she hadn't a care in the world. The fireflies were all dancing about in the air around her as if she was controlling them. Harriet felt happy for once and was deeply enjoying this wonderful moment.

From the village the children were looking down at her and had attracted some of the other villagers to witness this spectacle from afar. Vespera, having heard a commotion, went towards the other villagers to investigate. As she neared the villagers, they noticed her coming and fell silent, scuttling backwards, parting a small path for her to walk through. When she saw Harriet in the field below she quickly cast a ball of Light in each palm and brought them above her head and clapped her hands together. A giant Light beacon emitted from her hands pulsing its way through the air - it was the signal used every night to tell people to return home to the village before the sun set- and the fireflies disappeared back into the forest. Harriet, now alone again, walked up to the village where her mother was waiting for her at the top of the path.

"I am terribly sorry to of ruined your fun Harriet, but it is getting late now and the others were watching you."

"It is OK... I am used to it now," said Harriet miserably.

"Do not let it get to you my darling, they are just jealous of how good you are. Do not take it to heart. One day they will appreciate how special you really are and wonder why they ever treated you like this."

"I should not have to prove myself to them mother, I care not of what they think of me."

"Good girl, that is the spirit. Come, I shall make some tea before the trail." Harriet and her mother walked back to their hut and Harriet held her hand.

"Thank you Mother."

Chapter 2 - The Final Trial

The bright golden sun was beginning to set, casting a wash of red, orange and purple hues through the evening sky. As it set it cast a shadow in the shape of the forest that was encroaching on the village with each passing minute. Up in the village Vespera was about to perform the daily ritual of Lighting the giant lantern. The ritual had been performed every night since the Darkness was locked away -it was a precaution and was comforting for the villagers peace of mind. The people of the village still had a fear of that fateful time and wished for it to never happen again, so every evening the head of the village would summon the Light to protect them through the Dark hours of the night. Only the head of the village possessed the power to illuminate this ancient lantern as it was a rite of passage passed down by the Spirit of Light which no one else knew how to perform.

The ritual attracted all the villagers outside of their homes to gather round the lantern, watching Vespera intently, awaiting the spectacle that was about to unfold.

"Everyone please stand back and give me some room," she said to the villagers.

"Sorry ma'am," the villagers said as they scuffled backwards, kicking up a small cloud of dust at their feet. Harriet was stood close next to her mother as this ritual really excited her as the light was so intense and it made her feel at home.

"Harriet dear, can you please stand back. I know you enjoy it but I need space and privacy. You know this spell cannot befall any other ears but my own," Harriet moved away to stand with the villagers sheepishly.

"I apologize mother."

Vespera clasped her hands together and under her breath chanted the spell of Summoning. For this ritual to work, it required a great deal of power and a special, ancient spell which no one but the Elders understood. As Vespera began the spell, her hands beamed with Light and then like a vacuum sucking up dust, they began sucking in all the Light Spirit she had summoned. Harriet and the villagers looked up to the sky and saw the Light Spirit approaching. The spectacle looked like millions of fireflies racing towards the village from all directions- filling the sky with tiny specs of bright Light. As they got closer to the village they all flowed down towards Vespera's hands filling her entire body with an ethereal Light. As the last specs of Light filled her, she placed her hands on the lantern and the Light from her body began to transfer into it -she was a conduit for the Light Spirit. The Light that encased her body was rising from her feet, up her body, down her arms and out through her hands, until it was fully transferred. The lantern was pulsating, like a motor needing a kick-start. With her hands still firmly on the lantern she chanted "Lēoht" and a second later the lantern burst into a blinding Light that formed a bubble, growing and expanding from the lantern outwards into the air, getting larger by the second. Within this bubble of Light tiny specs of Light Spirit were swirling around making it look alive. As the Light grew it passed through the lanterns hanging from the huts and surrounding the village, igniting them with their own individual Light. The bubble of Light continued to grow bigger and bigger, illuminating all of the lanterns down the pathway -which resembled an airport runway- until it reached the edge of the forest, igniting the lanterns surrounding its outskirts simultaneously. The village was now encased in a huge shield of Light, reminiscent of a giant snow globe -a protective barrier devoid of all Darkness.

After this ritual had been performed, the villagers were usually forbidden to leave its protective barrier, but tonight was the only ever exception as it was the final Protector of Light trial. All of the children were gathered at the giant lantern dressed in their thick, warm, hooded cloaks whilst their parents were all wishing them the best of luck and instructing them to stay close to Vespera and Alucio at all times.

Harriet's mother spoke above the chatter.

"Now, the trial before you will test both your attack and defence skills to see if you can successfully stand up against the Darkness. I must remind you all that this is a very challenging and potentially dangerous trial if it is not adhered to correctly, so we will both be assisting closely to protect you should the need arise. We will be heading into the depths of the forest, where the Spirit of Darkness dwells."

A young child gasped in the crowd.

"*THE* Spirit of Darkness?! I thought he was locked away Miss?"

Harriet's mother turned to this child who was only about five years old and was now clinging to his mother's robe looking petrified.

"No my child, the spirit that took his place dwells in the forest, there is no danger from the corrupt Darkness anymore,"

The child hid behind his mother, pulling her robe over his face.

"Mummy, I am really scared."

A number of children were also looking petrified at the thought of this task, whilst others seemed to relish the challenge and were eager to get going.

"Now, I want you all to pay close attention to both of us and follow every word we tell you, there is no room for messing around or ignorance, so if you cannot abide to these rules then stay here in the comfort of your homes," Vespera said to the children.

"Before we head out, I want you all to summon your Lēoht armour as it is cold and very hard to see in the Dark," said Alucio sternly.

All of the children raised their hands above their heads and summoned up their Lēoht, pressing their glowing palms tightly together. They then pulled them apart making the Light stretch out like a sticky trail of honey. They brought their hands down their sides, palms facing to the ground, the Light was sticking to them, encasing their body in this armour of Light which keeps them warm and illuminates their path. Each of them now shining intensely like their skin itself was glowing.

"We are about to be leave the protective confines of the village," said Vespera, "So everyone be extra vigilant, stay with your partner and do not, under any circumstances, turn off your armour of Light!"

Harriet was stood near to her mother as she did not have a partner, but she was called to by Kira who was at the back of the group.

"Over here Harriet, come and partner up with me."

Harriet turned to her mother, "Do you mind if I go with Kira mother?"

"Of course not my love. Go, be with your friend," still feeling slightly awkward to this new concept of friendship, Harriet walked past the other children - who were already paired up and ready to go- and stood next to Kira.

"Hello Harriet, are you looking forward to this? I have never been out in the Dark like this before, I am quite excited about it."

"There is nothing to be excited about, it is cold, Dark and scary," Harriet replied.

"There is nothing to be afraid of, the corrupt spirit is locked away in the shrine so what harm could befall us?"

"I just do not like the Dark, it scares me."

"It scares you? But we have the power of Light in our possession. How can it scare you?" Kira asked.

"It just does. I do not trust it, I do not like it, and it scares me."

"I will protect you Harriet, do not be frightened," Kira stood sternly and assured her with a huge grin.

"Thank you Kira. But you do not know what is in the Darkness."

"What do you mean?"

"... Oh, never mind," Kira was curious what she meant, but before she could question Harriet, a booming voice yelled.

"Is everyone here?" bellowed Vespera.

"Yes Miss," "Here Miss," they replied.

"Good, then we shall begin. Everyone follow us and please keep up."

Vespera and Alucio turned around and began walking out of the village. The children were following closely behind, all talking amongst themselves and waving farewell to their family. Harriet had no one to wave to so she just kept her head down and walked on.

The Light emanating in the snow-globe-like shield was a subtle glow, as it was night time and the villagers needed sleep. The Light Spirit that was circulating the air allowed for no shadow to be produced within it. The children's armour of Light were adding extra illumination to the sky and their surroundings, brightening up the rocks and mud around their feet, but casting no shadows whatsoever.

As they were walking down the muddy hill following the long, winding pathway, Kira and Harriet were getting to know each other and discussing the trials from earlier that day.

"How you defeated the statue earlier was brilliant Harriet. The way you compressed the Light and tore it apart, I have never seen anything like that before!" Kira said.

"It is not that great..." Harriet felt embarrassed again as she was not used to people praising her abilities,

"I just like to practise new ways of controlling the Light and seeing what I can do with it."

"The power of it though...when it combined above the statue it was immensely potent. I could feel it in the air. I even heard the others saying how amazed they were by it."

"I doubt it. They only ever say bad things about me."

"They were, I swear, I would not lie to you Harriet."

The two children in front of them who were brother and sister, turned around quickly and whispered to Harriet.

"She is right Harriet, you were fantastic earlier," and they turned around hurriedly before anyone else noticed them talking to her.

Harriet could not believe what was going on, people were actually being nice to her, praising her instead of ridiculing and bullying her.

"See! Some people respect your powers, no matter how they treat you," Kira assured her.

"They have a strange way of showing it..."

As they continued the walk down the pathway, the field below was a wash of Light Spirit dancing all around the midnight air. The tree which Harriet was sat in earlier was once again filled with fireflies, whether it was for the trees shade or for comfort of Harriet's presence, they seemed to all gather at this tree every evening. It looked beautiful from afar, as if the very leaves on its old, worn branches were made of Light.

They approached the outskirts of the forest, the lanterns surrounding it were Lighting up the trees down the Dark pathway, making the forest look like a black and white picture, gradually fading out into complete blackness. Harriet's mother stopped at the barrier and turned to face the children, who were all trying to peek into the deep, Dark forest.

"OK everyone, we are now going to pass through the barrier of Light, once we are out in the forest you need to be careful where you step as this forest can be dangerous at night"

She turned back to face the barrier and placed her palms flat against it, once again chanting a spell too quietly for anyone else to hear. Light pulsed from her hands and the barrier began to ripple like a disturbed puddle. Alucio walked through it and stood on the other side of it awaiting the children to enter the forest.

"Everyone please walk through the Light and wait on the other side," said Vespera.

The children walked through the barrier of Light, some of them approaching it slowly, testing it with their hands before walking through it. Other children were leaping through and some walked through it totally unbothered by the excitement. As the children passed through, still wearing their armour of Light, they felt a huge drop in temperature,

"The Darkness is pleasantly cold is it not," said Alucio.

"Nu..nu..no itssss na..not it's f..f...freezing!" said a jitter- toothed child.

Harriet did not appear to feel the cold like the other children did. It may have been because her focus and attention was solely fixated elsewhere on two glowing spheres of Light, deep among the Darkness. She couldn't tell how near or far they were because the Darkness was so densely thick. They were faint and she could only just make them out, but they seemed like a huge pair of eyes watching her and the group.

She turned to her Mother.

"Mother, mother look, what is tha...?" but Vespera was busy concentrating on the path in front of them.

"Not now Harriet, this pathway can be dangerous at night," as Harriet looked back, whatever she saw glowing had now sunk back into the Darkness.

Every child was keeping an eye out for anything that stood out in the pitch black Dark of the night. Noises were heard in the air, like the Darkness was circling and surrounding them and some of the children grew nervous and scared.

"Do not be frightened children," said Vespera, "It is just the wind. The corrupt Darkness has long since been sealed away so there is no threat out here. The Spirit of Darkness lets us use parts of him as practise."

The forest was lit up from the brilliantly bright armour of Light surrounding them all, but the deeper into the forest they went, the Light began to lose its power like a flame being suffocated by black smoke.

"We are nearing where the Spirit of Darkness dwells, so please be extra cautious from here-on out, as the Darkness grows thicker the further we go and you might fall over something," said Vespera.

As they scrambled over the giant tree roots and piles of fallen leaves that were blocking the path, they reached an open clearing. Tall trees surrounded them and the floor was strewn with red, brown and yellow leaves with murky greens hidden underneath, which were illuminated under the glow of their armour.

"Here will do, we are deep enough for the trial," Vespera said to Alucio.

They stopped and turned to face the children who were all eager to find out what was happening.

"We are going to use this clearing as our trial ground. For those of you who are unaware of what is going to happen, we are going to be sealing a barrier around a portion of the Darkness Spirit. This will allow a controlled fight against the Darkness. The trial will test the Light powers we had you perform earlier today, but this time on a moving target."

Some of the children gasped, looking terrified.

"But Miss, what if the Darkness takes us?"

"We will be here to control it and we will not let anything happen to you, the Darkness will be surrounded by a special Light that it cannot breach. Please children, do not forget that this is not the corrupt Darkness, you have nothing to fear," said Vespera.

Alucio was stood in the middle of the clearing casting LightCraft no one had seen before. The Light he was summoning gave off no shine, it was like a dull piece of glass. It started collecting together in the air a few metres high and the Light Spirit was constructing it together like a jigsaw. It expanded, growing outwards and down until it reached the ground, creating a dome of Light in the clearing. Within the dome it was pitch black where it had surrounded the Darkness, Alucio then placed his hands on the dome and very slowly, the once dull looking structure illuminated gradually until the Darkness was forced to compress into a smaller shape, just floating within it like a cloud of smoke. Then two bright balls of Light appeared on it for eyes.

"Why does it have eyes like that Miss?" a child asked.

"Because the Dark needs the Light, just as the Light needs the Dark to exist. The eyes are its source of Light," she replied.

Harriet had paid no attention to this whole affair as her attention was focused elsewhere. She had seen those spheres of glowing Light again and was watching them intently. They seemed to be edging closer towards her, disappearing and reappearing as they moved closer. It must be moving among the trees Harriet thought. She was confused and highly intrigued as to what they were. Just as she was about to start walking towards them the children began to make some noise and she looked round to see what was going on.

The children all gasped in amazement.

"Whoa! That is amazing!" said a young girl.

"Arghh," screamed a frightened child.

"Do not be afraid. The dome my husband has just made has a sole purpose for sealing Darkness inside of it, it is perfectly safe. This is where you will fight a piece of Darkness," said Vespera.

"I will now demonstrate for you," said Alucio, "Within this dome you can fight with the Darkness and test your powers, it will be like a real fight so you must give it your all. I will stand guard in case you need to escape or you get hurt," He turned and walked through the dome, the Light bent around his body and let him pass through.

"Now children I want you all to pay close attention to the movements of the Darkness," Alucio said whilst readying himself to attack it. The children were now silent watching on in anticipation. Alucio launched balls of Light at the Darkness and it moved around like a cloud of smoke on the wind to avoid his assault.

"Can you not hit it?" shouted one of the children cockily.

"Enough of that!" Vespera said to the child.

Alucio smirked having heard this and let out a barrage of Light attacks cutting right through the Darkness, splitting it up into pieces. But the Darkness merged back together again as one.

"What has happened Miss, why did it rejoin like that?" asked Kira.

"That is because of the dome Alucio has set up, the Darkness is stuck inside of it unable to escape, so it can easily rejoin itself back together."

The Darkness was now attacking Alucio, jutting out huge spikes of black from its smoke like body which Alucio was deflecting away using a Light shield, counter attacking with Light balls to break it up once more.

"Are you watching children? This is how you fight the Darkness Spirit," Vespera said to them.

Alucio stopped fighting and stepped out of the dome.

"There you go children. That is how it is done. Please follow my lead and do your best. We will be right outside watching you."

"Now who would like to try?" Vespera asked them, "Anyone?" but none of the children had the courage to attempt it first.

Kira piped up, "I will Miss."

"Very well Kira. Please step through and begin your attack," She lifted her arm up gently, pointing to the dome. Kira nodded to her and walked over to where Alucio was standing.

"Just walk straight through it Kira," he said pointing at the dome of Light.

She passed through it and the Light wrapped around her body -like she was sinking into a pool of water. Kira hastily readied herself; her hands were sparking with Light Spirit as the Darkness lunged forward in an attempt to knock her over.

"Whoa!" she shouted as she raised her hands to block.

She skidded back slightly on the loose soil and thrust her hands out, pushing the Darkness away from her. She fired off a series of Light bolts at the Darkness to stun it, and then began to rub her palms in a circular motion making her disc of Light, throwing it towards the Darkness slicing it in half. The disc was bouncing off of the dome like a bouncy ball, repeatedly cutting the Darkness into smaller pieces.

"That is enough Kira," said Alucio, "Very good indeed."

Kira stepped out of the dome. The children clapped for her as she approached them.

"Well done Kira, that was excellent," said Vespera.

"Thank you Miss," she looked over to Harriet, "Your turn next Harriet!" Kira shouted cheekily. Harriet looked slightly scared and felt put on the spot.

"Are you ready Harriet?" Her mother asked her.

"Uhm... not really Mother," she replied.

"It will be alright Harriet."

"Ok. I will go next then," she was wary about going in the dome with the Darkness Spirit and walked slowly towards her father.

"Come on Harriet, no need to be afraid. I will be right here with you," he assured her.

"But I am scared father, I do not like the Dark."

"You will be fine little one, I believe in you."

She looked up at him, and then looked at the Darkness hovering inside the dome, biting her bottom lip and curling her face up with worry.

"Walk through the dome Harriet," her father said.

She very slowly edged her way over to it, not taking her eyes off the Darkness within. She went inside. The Darkness Spirit which had been hovering idly looking around the forest, now instantly turned its full

68

attention to Harriet, glaring its bright eyes directly at her. Before she even had a chance to ready herself it attacked her like a feral dog, ravaging her with such brute force, sending her flying down to the floor. Harriet was stunned and dazed, she had no room to attack this menacing beast as it was wrapping its long streams of Darkness around her body, lifting her up into the air like a rag doll.

She was shouting for help.

"Father help me!"

Alucio charged in, pulling her from the clutches of the Darkness, throwing her out of the dome onto the floor. She picked herself up and walked away towards her mother, stopping mid way to turn and look at her father who was now face to face with this monster.

The Darkness seemed agitated and began to move about erratically, seemingly angry at him, but he stood still, staring at it, his hands clenched as he took a stance in readiness for its attack. He opened his hands and his palms were glowing a fierce white. As the Darkness whooshed around like a snake of smoke trying to distract its opponent it thrust forwards towards him, he raised his hands making a barrier of Light which deflected it's attack, but the force from it sent him skidding backwards, disturbing the ground he stood on, kicking up leaves and soil in the air. The children were watching on with bated breath, none of them had seen anything like this before and they couldn't believe their eyes. Alucio was casting off balls of Light from each hand; as he closed his fist and opened it the compressed Light took form of a ball which he hurled towards the Darkness. The impact tore off a section of it and it started to drift off like a wisp of smoke from a burnt out fire. But then something happened which even Vespera and Alucio could not foresee. The torn off piece of Darkness Spirit now had its own set of eyes and there were now two of these beings fighting Alucio. Her mother gasped and immediately ran over to assist him.

Something was wrong she thought to herself, this should not be. As she ran towards him she was firing off Light Spirit at the dome trying to help, but they deflected off it.

She shouted at Harriet.

"Harriet, watch the children."

As she got near to the dome, the two Darkness beings merged back together as one, growing bigger than it was before. The huge eyes of this piece Darkness were steaming white. Harriet's mother shouted at the top of her lungs.

"GET OUT OF THERE ALUCIO!" but as the words left her mouth the Darkness had over powered him and swallowed him amongst its pitch black figure, encasing his entire body in Darkness.

The Darkness drew away from his body a few moments later and was lingering behind him in the air. Streams of Darkness were latched onto Alucio connecting him to the Darkness like a puppet on stings.

He was held up in the air, limp and lifeless with a pair of glowing white eyes.

"Oh no...NO...my darling... what have you done to my husband you monster?!" she cried.

The Darkness turned to face Vespera and spoke to her through her husband's body. The sound was so deep and deafening that it shook the very ground they stood on, making the dome of light quiver.

"He is the sacrifice needed for my return."

"You will NOT take my husband you abomination!" she threw LightCraft towards the Darkness with a ferocious strength, but it just bounced off the dome of Light as if it was nothing.

"Your shrine is weak. You think a mere seal by you petty humans will cage a spirit such as myself? Ha... ha... ha... you will all get what is coming to you for what you did to me all those years ago."

Harriet had been watching on without batting an eyelid, her face was a wash of anger and sadness; tears streamed down her face as she clenched her teeth, making her cheeks throb. 'Why was this happening to her father?' she thought.

Her mother was still screaming and attacking the barrier with no hope of aiding her husband.

Harriet took a breath and walked towards the Darkness.

"Harriet, get back!" but Harriet walked on in silent determination, eyes set solely on the beast before her.

Now standing in the clearing between her mother and the Darkness, she just stood there whilst her mother screamed for her to get back. Harriet stood calmly with her arms down by her sides, closed her eyes and turned her palms to face upwards. Particles of light began to flow from the air around her, sinking into her palms, their intensity grew with every second. The Light was coming from as far as you could see, dodging the trees and children like a fast moving current flowing directly into her palms. Harriet was sucking every spec of Light from the world into her and a glow began to encase her entire body until it became so bright and intense that she disappeared within the brightness. The Light then sank into her body, and for a few short moments -which felt like minutes- it became so Dark it was as if there was no Light left in the world except for the beading eyes of the Darkness and her father. Then in a split second, a burst of Light exploded out of the Dark sending leaves spewing through the air, and a glowing figure with an immensely bright white body, eyes and wings appeared. Harriet was nowhere to be seen. Light was flowing around this figure, or more accurately put, this figure was made of Light.

Harriet's mother gasped.

"No..."

"So... you have come out to play then?" The Darkness bellowed through Alucio.

74

The wings of this angelic figure expanded out like a gracious eagle, their span was as huge as a branch of the tallest tree.

"Be gone," this winged figure said as it flapped its huge wings downwards with such fierce force, sending a massive surge of Light racing towards the Darkness. Its voice was like a calm, mother gently singing a lullaby to her baby.

The Light pierced straight through the Darkness, sending both Alucio and the Dark demon soaring through the air. The Darkness was being torn apart by the Light and disintegrating into nothingness.

"This is not the end!" it said just before it vanished.

Alucio collided hard with a tree and fell face down to the ground. The children looked on in terror, horrified at what they were seeing. Vespera got up off her knees, wiped the tears from her face and ran towards her husband who was now lying on the floor motionless at the foot of a tree. The Darkness had no control over him now and had left his body. She shook him and he started to stir.

Through blurry eyes he caught a glimpse of the ethereal figure standing before him.

"Is... th... that... h... her?" he was struggling to speak.

"Yes my love... yes it is," she said, sobbing and holding his hand tight as she told him.

"I am... so sorry honey... I... endangered you... and the... children."

"It is OK my dear, it is gone now, it is not your fault."

"I am... so... sorry"

"You could not have known that would happen. At least none of the children were injured or worse..."

"But... Harriet..."

They both looked towards the shimmering winged figure which was Lighting up the entire forest.

"So, she is the one," Vespera said, "I always knew in my heart it was her, but I never wanted to believe it."

The figure began to flicker on and off like a broken Light bulb for a few seconds and then it went out entirely, leaving Harriet standing in its place. The forest had fallen pitch black and everyone cast a Lēoht, gently Lighting the forest up again once more. Harriet swayed side to side slightly for a moment and then collapsed on the ground.

"HARRIET!" her mother screamed as she ran over to her unconscious body.

All the children gathered around Vespera who was now cradling Harriet in her arms. "What happened Miss?"

"Is she going to be ok?"

"What was that thing that came to save us?"

"Is that monster coming back?"

Vespera composed herself.

"Please children not now. I shall explain everything to you all later. We must get back to the village as fast as possible."

Vespera lifted Harriet off the ground and carried her limp body in her arms.

"Now all of you make haste. Keep your Lēoht at full brightness and stay close together as we head home."

The children huddled together, utterly terrified. With Lēoht's shining bright they began walking back to the village with their questions eagerly awaiting an answer.

Vespera and Alucio were walking side by side and a little way behind the children so they could keep a keen eye on them. He whispered in her ear as they were walking so the children would not hear.

"You know what this means my love?"

"Of course I do," she softly responded "But for now, we cannot let it get to us. There is more at stake than our compassion, as much as it pains me to say it."

They both looked down at Harriet, with a face so peaceful it was as if she was having the best dream in the world, completely unaware of what was going on around her. They wondered if she had any idea what was going to happen to her. Of course she didn't, only they knew what fate awaited her, and everyone else for that matter.

"We still have a while until we reach the barrier, keep your wits about you, we are not out of the Dark just yet," Harriet's mother said to the children.

Since the appearance of the winged being the forest had fallen silent and still, like a petrified mouse being hunted by a bird.

When they finally reached the edge of the forest, the sun was rising behind the village making it a silhouette of black, against the rising orange sun. The rays of sunlight were casting their way through the mist from the cold night, catching the particles of Light lingering in the air and making them glisten.

As daylight was breaking and they were back in the confines of the protective shield, the group edged ever closer to their homes knowing that the Darkness was gone and they were safe. For now...

Chapter 3 – Invīsibilis

Three days had passed since the Darkness attacked them in the forest and in that time nearly half of the villagers had disappeared.

The morning dew had settled on Harriet's face making her glisten like a beautiful statue. Her eyes opened slowly as she let out a giant yawn, stretching her arms out -which were sore and hurt for some reason. She pulled back her cold damp bed sheets, slid her legs over the edge of the bed and sat up. Still half asleep she brushed the moistness from her face, gasping in pain at the touch. Now she was conscious she realised that her skin was in more pain than she could bear and it was throbbing like her blood was trying to force its way out. The soreness was like severe sunburn and it hurt her too much to touch. She held out her hands to look at them, turning them over slowly, assessing the cause of the pain. Her palms were bright red with hints of purple from where they were beginning to bruise and the bruising was growing up her arms and onto her face and her entire body looked like she had been mildly burnt. 'How did this happen?' Harriet wondered.

She could hear the villagers outside making quite a racket, so she got up, slipped on her shoes, and as the morning was unpleasantly cold and she wanted to hide these mysterious burns, she picked up her robe and put it on carefully, trying to ignore the pain. She pulled the hood over her head to hide her bruised face. Still sleepy she walked towards the door, dragging her feet along the floor in agony, but determined to see what all the commotion was about.

As she opened the door her hand stung from the contact of the wooden frame and the bright Light from the sun and loudness of the villagers was a shock to her senses. She pulled her hood down over her face to shade her eyes from the suns glare. Now she was able to see, she saw all of the villagers gathered together and noticed they were all talking to her mother simultaneously. She wondered what was going on. 'Had something bad happened?' Harriet was not sure.

Among the many voices she made out someone shouting.

"The Darkness, it has returned!"

Vespera then raised her voice above them all.

"People... I understand your fear. I understand you are scared. But you cannot let fear control you, that is exactly what the Darkness wants."

"But the Darkness is back and is growing stronger by the minute," said a worried villager.

"This is nothing to be afraid of. All we must do is increase the power of the shrine's seal and banish the part of Darkness that has escaped," said Harriet's Mother.

"But the others... they have not returned from their pilgrimage. How are we to know if they succeeded or not?" a scared villager asked.

"This time we will send our most powerful Sorcerers. My husband will be going this time to make sure that it works and that we are safe. Now, please return to your homes and begin making preparations," said Harriet's Mother.

Harriet still had no idea what they were talking about. She draped the sleeves of her robe over her hands and covered her face with her hood even more so than it already was so that no one could see her bruises. As she walked through the crowd of rowdy people towards her mother, the villagers became aware of Harriet's presence among them and fell silent at the very sight of her. Harriet heard them whispering to each other.

"She is awake."

"I did not think she would have woken up from that."

The villagers started crowding around to thank her. She had no idea what was going on. 'What is everyone thanking me for?' she thought to herself, all the more confused at the situation.

"Thank you for protecting my son."

"Thank you Harriet, I am truly grateful for what you did."

"I do not know what you are thanking me for," Harriet replied to them.

"Do not be so modest, you did a very brave thing Harriet, we all owe you so much."

"Please, let her be and return to your homes," Harriet's mother said to them, "She has endured enough as it is."

They stopped fussing over her and went back to their homes, looking back over their shoulders smiling at Harriet with gratitude. The village fell silent. Harriet, now even more confused, walked up to her Mother and asked her what was happening.

"It is nothing to worry about my dear. Last night one of the villagers noticed the Darkness breaking through the Light barrier. There must be a weak spot in it but it is nothing to worry about."

Harriet knew her mother was lying to her, something must be seriously wrong for her to lie.

"Mother, please do not lie to me. I am covered in bruises, my skin hurts, and the villagers actually spoke to me for once and thanked me for something I do not remember!"

"Do you not remember anything at all my darling?"

"No, only father being controlled by the Darkness."

"Well you have been asleep for three days, your memory must be a little weak."

"Three days?! Are you serious?"

"You were exhausted and unconscious. If you want the truth Harriet, you saved us all."

"What? How? I do not understand what is going on mother."

"That is all you need to know my dear, you saved us all from the Darkness in the forest."

"Why are you not telling me everything?!" Harriet shouted.

"Now my dear, please do not be angry with me. First I must tend to your burns. We cannot leave you like that now can we?"

"No... It is so painful mother, I want it to stop."

"Come Harriet, let us go back home and I shall make you better."

They walked back to their hut together through the silent village. The villagers were peeking out of their doors and windows at Harriet and she could see them in the corner of her eye as she peered out from the shadow of her hood.

"Mother, why is everyone staring at me?" she whispered.

"You protected their children and they are extremely thankful to you."

"But I do not remember doing it."

"You summoned an extraordinary amount of Light Harriet, your body is not used to sustaining that amount of Light Spirit, that is why you have a loss of memory from that night."

"I did?"

"Yes. I will tell you everything later. First we must go inside."

Her mother opened the door and let Harriet walk in before her, still struggling to walk with her body in complete agony. As they entered their home, the pain Harriet was in meant that she could only sit awkwardly on her bed. Her mother closed the heavy door gently then helped Harriet undress so that she could tend her burns.

"Ouch!" Harriet yelped, as her mother took off her robe. It rubbed against her sore skin.

"I am sorry my love, we need to remove your clothes for this. Your friend Kira visited you whilst you were asleep you know. I am glad you have a friend that cares for you." She said, smiling at her daughter.

"Did she?"

"Yes my love. She sat with you for a while each day hoping you would wake," Harriet looked bashful.

As her mother finished undressing her Harriet saw the burns on her bare body for the first time.

"It looks horrible mother. I look so ugly," she sobbed slightly.

"Do not say such things Harriet, you are a beautiful girl. This is only a burn from Light Spirit, it will disappear. I have had it before too."

"Really, when was that?" Harriet asked.

"Back when I was around your age. I was learning some potent LightCraft from a parchment that was passed down to me from my mother. I could not quite master it at the time and the Light Spirit overwhelmed and burnt me many times."

"Really? I cannot imagine you being unable to master the Light."

"I was once a just a child of the Light just like you, long before I was an Elder of Light. But you are far stronger than I was at your age Harriet."

"I do not believe that. You are the most powerful sorceress of Light I have ever known."

"One day you will see Harriet. Now sit comfortably on the edge of your bed please, I need to begin treating your burns."

Vespera stood up and put her hands gently in the air in front of her, palms level with her shoulders, facing towards Harriet.

"This will be cold my love, but please do not fight it or you will not heal as quickly."

She whispered a chant too quiet for Harriet's ears to hear and miniature specs of Light began to surface from out of her palm -like water dripping down from a condensation filled ceiling- and jumped out onto

Harriet's bare skin like tiny fleas. They latched onto her bruised body and dissolved into small puddles on her skin, merging with the other small puddles of Light that were now forming all over her body.

"It. It is so.....so....c.c...ooolddd.." Harriet said through chattering teeth, shivering all over.

"Accept it, let it soothe your body."

Harriet was now completely covered -except for her eyes, mouth and nose holes for breathing- in a film of Light and she looked like a polished brass ornament. Her shivering made it ripple like water.

"This will stay on you until your body absorbs up all of the Light. I shall make you some tea to warm you up after."

She emptied out some water from a small wooden bucket. The bucket had a thick woven rope as its handle that draped onto the floor. She poured the water into the cauldron and lit beneath it by using Light Spirit. The Light was moving around really fast, emulating heat. This was how the villagers kept warm, cooked their food and heated their water. Light Spirit was truly a wonderful thing.

After a short while -enough time to heat up a huge cauldron of water- Harriet's body had soaked up all of this cold Light, and her burns and bruising had vanished.

"I cannot feel the pain any more mother. I never knew you could do that with Light Spirit," she said as she put her clothes back on, still numb and shivering from the cold.

"There are many things that you do not know my child. The time has come for me to share something with you," she stepped over to her bed and lifted up the sheet, dragging out an extremely old wooden box from beneath it. The box brought out a huge pile of dust which swirled and gathered all around them. The markings on the box were hand carved and deeply ground into the wood. Harriet noticed that it was the language of the Light.

"That parchment I spoke of earlier Harriet, I now give it to you. It is yours, learn it well."

"Wow, really? This box looks so old. How old is this mother?"

"Older than me that is for sure," she giggled to herself, making Harriet laugh as well.

"Thank you mother, this is great. But what will it teach me?"

"I cannot say any more. The rule of this parchment is to learn it yourself. Only then are you are worthy of the teaching it holds."

"How exciting!"

Harriet was beaming with joy, she loved LightCraft more than anything and an entirely new crafting was the best thing she could wish for.

"Thank you so much mother, I feel honoured."

She handed Harriet a nice warm pot of tea - recently picked from the local fields- she had freshly brewed.

"Drink this, it will warm you up."

Harriet reached out and took the hot cup from her mother, warming her cold hands "Thank you mother."

The sunlight was casting its rays through the tiny window in their hut, reflecting the dust lingering in the air as Harriet sipped slowly on her tea.

"The sun will be setting soon," Harriet said as she gazed out of the window.

"How are you feeling now my darling, I hope the tea is helping?"

"I feel fine thanks mother, it is warming me up."

"Good girl, I think we should get some rest, it has been a busy day. Tomorrow we must send more people to reinforce the shrine and we have to make some supplies for your father.

"I am OK. I have been asleep for three days. What do you mean sending people to the shrine?"

"Oh you do not know what has happened do you. Well... Since the forest incident three days ago, the Darkness has been growing in power and the seal on the shrine is weakening. So villagers have been going on a pilgrimage to the shrine to try and restore its power."

Harriet was gazing at her mother in bewilderment.

"However, the problem is we do not actually know how the Darkness escaped its prison in the first place, or whether our efforts are having any benefit. I am afraid none of the villagers have returned to tell us..." she said and she gazed through the window with a distant, worried look on her face.

Harriet noticed her mother's expression and became concerned.

"No one has returned? What do you think has happened to them?" but her mother avoided the question.

"The sun is beginning to set, please excuse me for a little while Harriet, it is time to Light the lantern."

"...OK mother. I will stay here and drink my tea," she noticed that her mother had avoided her question.

As she opened the door she stopped and looked at Harriet who was busy sipping her tea, the vapour was steaming her face and Harriet had her eyes closed enjoying the warmth.

"Try and read the parchment. I will see how you have progressed when I return," she shut the door, leaving Harriet alone on her bed.

Harriet put her pot of tea on the ground and opened the dusty old box; a beige coloured cloth was laid over the top of the parchment to protect it. She removed the cloth to reveal the parchment that was laid underneath, wearily picking it up out of its housing she gazed at its beauty, scared that it would break in her hands. She unrolled it slowly, revealing its secrets inch by inch. The parchment was covered in a series of images around the outside edges of it and in the middle was an outline of a person with a strange looking glow surrounding them. The only problem was that Harriet had no idea how to read this as she had never been taught the Language of Light, it was only for the Elders to know.

She ran her fingers around the edge of the parchment, turning it over in her hands whilst looking at each of these illustrations that were drawn onto it. As she got around to the last corner she realised it was a story made up of images, like an instruction. But she did not understand what it meant or how she could decipher it. The shapes on the parchment were silhouetted shapes, so she thought maybe try and make these shapes with her hands, but this did not work. She used the Light Spirit to make these shapes out of Light in the air but this did not work either. She cast Lēoht whilst forming the shapes with her hands, and once again this did nothing. She grew tired and agitated, so she lay her weary body down in her bed staring at the straw ceiling. She let thoughts tick through her head trying to understand it all, all the while still absentmindedly making hand shapes in the air.

Just when she was about to stop and have a sleep, she noticed a Light shadow cast on the wall -a Light shadow is a different tone of Light that replicates a shadow- faintly resembling a shape she recognised. Harriet brightened her Lēoht, making the Light shadow stand out stronger, it was a letter! A burst of excitement rushed through her, making her back tingle and her hairs stand on end. She sat up forgetting her aches for a moment, eagerly working through all of the images one by one, casting a Light shadow then writing down the letter displayed on the wall until she had figured out the encryption. She wrote the letters down on the piece of cloth that was in the box protecting the parchment, using Light Spirit from her fingertip as an ink-like substitute, scribing bright, illuminated writing into the raggedy old cloth. Once she had written all of the letters Harriet looked at the cloth to see what it said.

The parchment read; To go unseen 'Invīsibilis'

Invīsibilis? Go unseen? Harriet didn't know what it meant, but she was excited. She stood up from her bed, gave herself some space and followed the instructions in an attempt to try it out. She cast Lēoht then chanted "Invīsibilis," but nothing happened. She thought perhaps she had deciphered it incorrectly, so she went through all of the letters again, but she had written it correctly. Harriet approached it a different way, this time chanting "Invīsibilis," before she cast Lēoht, again nothing happened except a bright Light appearing as usual. Once more she attempted it, but this time chanting "Invīsibilis," at the exact moment she cast

Lēoht. Something happened this time, the Light that usually radiated from her hands did not appear, and instead a transparent, watery-looking Light had formed in her palms. It sank around her hands like a glove and began to work its way up her arms, her face and over her entire body covering her in this fluid-like Light, similar to the one her mother had just used to heal her burns. However, this one felt different, it sat heavier on her skin like she was wearing a body suit. She looked down at her hands, they weren't there. She could not believe her eyes, she was actually looking right through her own body, it was as if she was just a pair of eyes and nothing more.

Harriet screamed.

"Arghh my hands!" she was scared for a moment until she realised that this Light around her body was making her invisible.

"I am invisible?!" she yelled in her head with amazement.

The sunlight had nearly vanished when the lantern outside burst alive, filling Harriet's hut with Light Spirit swirling around in the air. The Light flowed towards Harriet and landed on her now invisible skin, covering her in a silky looking layer of Light -like rain on a window catching the sun's rays- making her almost visible.

Her mother opened the door and the Light Spirit that landed on Harriet quickly left her and returned to the air around her, leaving her invisible once again.

"Harriet I am back, how do you feel?" she glanced at the bed, noticing Harriet was gone and the parchment was left out in the open.

"Harriet you cannot leave this out, anyone could find it," she said aloud to herself, completely unaware that Harriet was still in the room with her.

Harriet was so excited that she couldn't contain herself and she accidentally bumped into the cauldron, spilling some hot water on her feet.

"Ouchhhh!" she yelled, making her mother jumped in shock.

"Harriet?" she called.

Harriet was now only slightly transparent as she had lost her focus. Her Invīsibilis was fading, making her appear like a ghostly figure until it faded out completely and returned her back to normal.

"Harriet! You... learned that already!?" Vespera gasped.

"Yes mother, it was not too hard, I figured it out shortly after you left. It is AMAZING!" she shrieked, "Thank you so much, I can have soooo much fun with this!" her face was beaming with joy.

"Astonishing, this took me weeks to decipher. You did it in that space of time? Incredible."

"It took you weeks mother, really? But it was so easy."

"This is not to be shown to anyone Harriet, do you understand? This is a powerful form of LightCraft that is passed down from the Elders. It is for you, and you alone, to have knowledge of."

But Harriet was not listening properly, she was too busy playing with this newly learned LightCraft, making only her arms and legs vanish, giggling in amazement at her floating body and head.

"You truly are a gifted child Harriet... it is no surprise that the Light has chosen you."

Harriet having heard this stopped what she was doing and looked to her mother.

"What do you mean the Light has chosen me?"

"The Spirit of Light chooses who she wishes to take under her wing so to speak, and it seems that you are the next one she wants. It is the first step on the path of becoming an Elder."

Harriet's mouth dropped open and her eyes went as wide as an owl.

"She wants... me? An Elder, but how, why, I do not..."

"Harriet, do not worry about the how and why. It is an Elders decision to pass the rite to a chosen 'Child of Light' who has been deemed worthy enough. That is all I can tell you, the rest is up to you to figure out along the way, all I can do is illuminate your first steps."

"I...do not understand? How am I to begin, when I do not know how or what I am supposed to do?"

"The Light Spirit will guide you along the path of the Elder."

"...OK mother, I am still very confused though."

"All will become clear my child, all will become clear."

Harriet felt overwhelmed at what her mother was telling her, all the more excited by the new LightCraft power she had discovered.

"Do you mind if I go outside and try my new LightCraft out mother?"

"Of course not, go out and play my darling, just do not let anyone see you using it whatever you do!"

"I will not be foolish. I will go down to the fields, everyone should be in their homes by now anyway."

"Be safe and do not be out too late."

"Thank you mother. I will be back shortly."

Harriet slipped on her shoes and opened the door where the Light Spirit was ablaze from the lantern. She poked her head out to scan around for anyone still lingering around in the village, but it seemed that nobody was out. Once she made sure the coast was clear she snuck quickly behind her house and down the hillside, her feet gave way underneath her amongst all the loose soil and she skidded down the muddy slope, landing on the pathway a few feet below. She brushed the dirt off herself and decided that the best place for practising this Invīsibilis LightCraft was in her tree amongst all of the fireflies, as she would be concealed from sight by their intense glow.

As Harriet got closer to the tree, the fireflies began to fly towards Harriet like they were being magnetised to her. She thought that this would pose a problem if they landed on her like they normally do, as it would show anyone looking down on the field that Harriet was there. So Harriet knelt behind a rock on the hill, out of anyone's line of sight from the village and cast Invīsibilis. The fluid-like Light once again took over her body and made her invisible. The fireflies stopped flowing towards her and began dancing in the air as they were before they noticed her.

"It really works" she said to herself as she carried on walking down to her tree. Harriet noticed the fireflies were flying away really fast in the opposite direction, like a flock of birds. She looked past them and stopped dead in her tracks because she had seen something, something monstrous at the edge of the forest.

Chills ran all over her body making her quiver. The Darkness she briefly recalled from three nights ago was just on the other side of the Light barrier. It was enormous now, almost as big as the trees that surround it, it had no shape, just a gigantic, intensely black mass with eyes a fierce white that looked like they gave off a trail of steam when they moved. The Darkness was drifting around the outskirts of the forest among the trees keeping away from the Light of the lantern, watching the village. Harriet was terrified, she dare not move. She did not want it to notice her so she just stayed perfectly still and watched it. She was glad to have this invisible LightCraft at her disposal or she would be out in the open.

Harriet was frozen stiff. It felt like an hour went by. The Darkness did nothing but stare at the village. Its breathing was so deep and haunting -like a scary old man with a blocked, raspy throat- Harriet could feel it rumble the ground beneath her feet. It scanned the area once more, shifting its white eyes around smoothly in the air, left to right, as if it was seeking something. It seemed like it could not find what it was looking for and turned around, sinking back into the Darkness from where it came.

Harriet waited until it was gone from her sight - although it was impossible to see anything in the black of the night- her eyes were still fixed on where it was hovering, she felt like she hadn't blinked in all the time she was there. Once she had stopped shaking in fear she let out a huge sigh of relief. Petrified and covered in goose bumps she quickly walked back towards the village, constantly looking all around her for any signs of it still lingering in the Dark. Her walk quickly became a run as she was desperate to be in the safe confines of her hut with her mother. She ran up the pathway so fast, tripping over her own feet and falling face first on the floor, covering herself in dirt. She quickly stood up and continued running up the path. Just before she reached the village, she heard a faint voice being carried on the wind in the distance- the most horrifying sound she had ever encountered.

"Harrrrrriiiiiiiiiieeeeeeeettttttttt..."

She could not move. Standing in fear, chills running up her back and onto her face she realised that her Invīsibilis had faded out without her noticing. Harriet moved only her eyes left to right looking around her, too petrified to move any limb of her body. She turned around slowly to look down to the field. Her eyes went as wide as they could physically go and her mouth fell open. Goosebumps ravaged her body so much that they stung her skin. There in the forest, the Darkness had returned and was staring directly at her with its gigantic menacing eyes.

"I seeeee yooooooouuuuuu," it whispered in a deep scratchy voice that sounded like the crackle of an old record player.

Harriet was horrified. She could not move a muscle, even though her mind was screaming "Run! Run! Run!" all she could do was stare at the huge monster.

The Darkness began to move around the barrier towards her slowly, its eyes locked onto her with a sinister gaze. She gained the courage to finally move and run to her house, bursting through the door, flinging it open so hard it hit the wall and startled her mother. She quickly slammed it shut, leaning on the door holding it closed, trying to catch her breath, still shaking all over in fear.

"Harriet?" her mother asked "Whatever is the matter?"

Harriet was out of breath, panting, shaking and white with fear.

"Darkness...in the forest...huge eyes...watching...called...name..." she panted.

"Harriet slow down. I do not know what you are saying,"

Harriet gained her breath, wiping the tears from her face as her mother knelt in front of her holding her hands.

"Tell me exactly what happened to you my dear."

Harriet took a deep breath and told her.

"I was walking down to the tree, but just before I got there I noticed this huge smoke like figure at the edge of the forest with these terribly bright, white eyes. From what I could see its body was almost as big as the trees in the forest."

"This is not good, not good at all... The Darkness has grown stronger. Are you OK Harriet? Did it see you?"

"No not at first, I had my Invīsibilis active. But I ran home so fast that I tripped and fell over. The Invīsibilis faded out without me realising and then I heard this awful voice calling my name, so I turned around and saw the Darkness staring right at me.

"It called your name?" her mother asked suspiciously.

"Yes it did, I was so scared mother, it sounded like it was after me. It was so loud that its voice shook the ground. It was staring right at me, it was horrifying." she started crying and her mother put her arms around her for comfort. Harriet squeezed her tight, crying into her robe.

"The pilgrimage must succeed tomorrow," Vespera whispered, "Or I fear it will be too late."

"We *can* seal it away again mother?"

"I hope so Harriet, I really do. Otherwise it will be like it was before."

Harriet yawned, she was exhausted and still ached slightly from the bruising.

"You should get some sleep Harriet. We have a busy day tomorrow."

"I will try to mother, but I do not know if I will be able to sleep now."

Harriet took off her robe and got into her bed as her mother was leaving the hut.

"Where are you going mother?"

"I need to speak to your father urgently, he is at Kira's house speaking to her parents. I will not be too long. Try to get some sleep my dear," she left the hut, leaving Harriet alone with her thoughts.

She got into bed and wriggled under the covers, still thinking about those huge eyes glaring at her and that terrifying voice calling to her. She was fighting to stay awake as she was so scared, but her eyes were so heavy that she drifted off to sleep almost instantly amidst all of her troubling thoughts.

Harriet did not sleep well that night. Not well at all.

Chapter 4 - The Pilgrimage

The following morning the entire village was busy preparing for the pilgrimage to the shrine; food and warm garments for the cold night were being made by everyone, and even the children were pitching in to help.

Harriet was helping her mother make a scrip of food for her father -a big leather pouch to hang around his waist- as she was extremely worried she would lose him and she wanted to do everything she could to help him, and if making him a nice meal was all she could do then she would do her best.

Vespera pulled a freshly baked loaf of bread from their stone oven that had been baked using LightCraft.

Harriet was yawning.

"Did you not sleep very well my dear?"

"No not at all, I kept having flashbacks of the Darkness staring at me, wondering if it was responsible for the villagers disappearing," she stopped what she was doing, casting a blank stare into thin air.

"Do not worry your little heart too much Harriet," her Mother said as she was kneading dough, "I am sure that whatever has happened to the other villagers will not happen to your father my dear."

"I... I suppose so..." said Harriet, "But... what if it does mother, the Darkness is out there, what if... what if he does not come back?" she held her head down a moment, looking sad, "What if they do not return? There will be no men left and no one except you is powerful enough to help seal the shrine."

"They will succeed, they are our best sorcerers."

"I just have a feeling deep inside of me mother, something is not right. I am scared for them, and for us."

She looked at Harriet with loving, worried eyes.

"Please do not worry Harriet. Let us finish making the supplies for your father, he will need them."

Harriet cut the warm bread into slices using a blade of Light that extended from her fingertips and she packed the Scrip with bread and fresh fruit and tied it up ready to give to her father.

There was a loud knock at the door.

116

"It is time," said a voice outside.

Harriet and Vespera went to go outside. As they stepped towards the door her mother put her arm out to stop her.

"Please do not mention anything about what you saw last night Harriet, we do not want to start a panic."

"I will not mother, but why?"

"The people need all the hope and strength they can muster for their pilgrimage. This will only dampen their resolve," she gave Harriet a hug and they left their hut.

Outside, the pilgrims were saying goodbye to their loved ones. One woman was in hysterics "Do not go! Please do not go my son!" she had already lost her husband and older son and all that was left was her youngest son who was about to go on his pilgrimage.

"But I have to mother, you know what we are tasked with, there is no escaping it," he said. "You are right my boy, I just do not know what I would do if I lost you too," she sobbed heavily and put her arms around her son.

Harriet looked all around her, the same thing was happening with each family and she realised that this was the

117

last group of male sorcerers the village had left to protect them. 'What was going to happen after this' she asked herself, 'what if this last glimmer of hope fades out like a dying Light?' She felt a shiver of fear up her spine and drew her hood over her head, tightened it even more so than usual and stood close to her mother and father. Harriet handed her father the leather scrip of food she had made him.

"Thank you Harriet, this will be a lovely meal," he said to her with a jolly smile.

"I had better go and join with the others now. See you soon my love," he said, giving Vespera a kiss on the cheek.

"Be safe my darling," she replied, putting on a brave face. Even though he was not showing it, she knew he was scared, and this frightened her the most.

Alucio turned to Harriet.

"Do not worry little one, I shall be back and if I can I will bring the lost ones back too." Harriet let a sad smile surface.

"Please... Please be careful father, I shall be waiting for your return. I will cook you your favourite meal when you get back."

"I will hold you to that promise little one," Alucio smiled then hugged them both.

Harriet was gripping on to his cloak as tightly as a cat clawing its paws into its owners skin. She realised that this could be the last time that she saw him. After they said their farewells, Alucio made his way over to the other pilgrims at the centre of the village.

Harriet was holding back her tears.

"Harriet?" a voice came through the crowd.

"Yes?" she responded to whomever it was.

"There you are, I have been meaning to speak to you," said Kira, who was dressed in a thick robe.

"What is the matter Kira, and what are you dressed like that for?"

"I have been asked to go on this pilgrimage. I wanted to tell you before I left."

"What? No! You cannot!" Harriet yelled at her.

"I will be OK Harriet. I have the strongest sorcerers in the village with me, nothing will happen to us." Kira reassured her.

"I have a really bad feeling about this Kira, please do not go. I cannot lose my only friend." Harriet's eyes were filling with tears and she was biting the inside of her bottom lip to stop herself from crying.

"I cannot go against the word of the village, you know that Harriet. I will see you when I get back. Take care of yourself whilst I am gone." she gave Harriet a big hug, Harriet was too limp to return the hug and just stood there, powerless to change the events that were about to unfold.

"Please be safe Kira," Harriet said as tears were looming heavily in her eyes.

"See you soon Harriet," Kira said as she walked over to join the pilgrims.

Once they had all said their farewells, the pilgrims lined up in a single file in the middle of the village. They all had cloaks with hoods made for them by their family, which were thickly woven with cotton and heavily lined with sheep's wool so that they could survive the cold temperature of the

Dark night. Each of them was holding a strong wooden staff with an orb at the tip, housed in a metal casing. They held their staffs in their left hands and with their right hands placed on the top of the orb they cast Lēoht and all the orbs filled with a brilliant bright glow that encased each of the pilgrims in a bubble of Light. The orbs had a stream of Light linking directly to the orb in front and behind them -like a stream of Lightning- binding them together. The Light now shone so bright that Harriet and the villagers had to shield their eyes to be able to see them.

And so began their pilgrimage. They started walking in unison down the path. All of the lanterns around the village, forest and path were lit up and the entire area was filled with a glow that soared high into the sky, even in the afternoon Light. As they walked on Harriet sat at the top of the path with her mother, surrounded by the rest of the village, anxiously watching them tread down the path to the forest.

"Mother..." Harriet said, her voice trembling with emotion.

"Yes my dear?"

"Are they going to return?"

"Of course they will Harriet. They are the strongest group we have,"

Harriet did not believe her. She figured her mother was only saying that to reassure the villagers who were around them.

"I am so worried. I wish I was going so that I could be with them."

"No Harriet. I need you here with me."

Harriet looked even more saddened now. She looked up to see that they were at the foot of the hill, about to pass through the barrier. The Light from their orbs was still blinding even at this distance.

As the pilgrims entered the forests mouth they disappeared out of sight. Harriet and the other villagers sat watching the forest long after the group had disappeared from sight in the hope that they would see some sort of resolution.

The Pilgrims were now in the forest, they instantly sensed that something sinister was lurking nearby. The wind began to rip the very fabric around them. The trees were shaking and cracking under the pressure of sustaining themselves against this fierce wind.

"This does not look good," said one of the pilgrims.

"Just keep moving," shouted Alucio.

They continued to press on. The wind speed increased and a thick Dark cloud began to emerge all around in the forest as far as they could see. They walked on but as they got deeper in the forest the cloud of smoke grew thicker and the Light began to deplete all around them.

"It is only afternoon, what is happening to the Light?" a pilgrim said.

"Something is not right," said another.

"Keep moving!" Alucio shouted, "We must make haste!"

"Yes sir!" they said, gaining focus once more.

Harriet and the villagers were still watching idly, completely unaware of the Darkness surrounding their loved ones. From where they sat the Light still appeared to be beaming through the afternoon sky and everything seemed to be as normal.

Suddenly Darkness shrouded the pilgrims and even their protective Lēoht lost its intensity. The Darkness was becoming stronger than the Light and all around them was nothing but a black abyss.

"Everyone stand back to back in a circle and keep an eye out, we must break through!" Alucio ordered. They stood in a circle, backs facing the middle so that they could see in a 360 degree view.

"We need to get to the shrine, let us move quickly," Alucio had to shout over the now gale force wind.

A loud rumbling sound emerged and the villagers trembled in fear.

"What is that sound?" Kira asked.

"The Darkness is here. Give it your all people," Alucio shouted.

Then suddenly from amidst the Dark, a pitch black mass of Darkness with humongous white eyes came charging at them with blistering speed.

"Attack!" roared Alucio, "Let us end this beast once and for all!"

They all cheered a huge battle cry and threw everything they had at the monster. Light was racing towards this beast ripping holes straight through it, but nothing seemed to slow it down or hurt it.

From the village they could see Light being thrown high into the treetops and the faint screams of battle could be heard even at that distance.

"Mother..." Harriet said worriedly.

"It is OK Harriet, they are strong," but they could see the Lights were becoming smaller in number and the noise of battle was fading. The villagers began to scream in fear and break down in panic. Terror ripped through them as they feared they had lost their loved ones.

"Everyone get to your homes, NOW!" Harriet's mother cried.

The villagers ran to their homes, some of them crying hysterically. Harriet stayed with her mother but she told her to go inside.

"Harriet I said go inside!"

"No! I am not going inside, I want to help them!" she was frantically screaming and crying in anger and began to unwillingly draw Light Spirit into her like she did in the forest.

"HARRIET! HOME, NOW!" Vespera shouted so loud that Harriet snapped out of it and the Light Spirit ceased to enter her body.

She went home looking completely devastated and sat on her bed, still crying and raging inside, feeling totally useless to do anything. She was curious as to what her mother was doing and why she was still outside, so she used her Invīsibilis and snuck outside again to see what it was. She saw her mother in a glowing state, perfectly still and focussed, then she disappeared and a ghostly apparition -like a clone of her mother made of Light flew up into the sky towards the forest- leaving a sparkly trail in the air behind her. Harriet was scared her mother would see her so she crept back into her hut and shut the door, hoping to see her from the window, but she was long out of sight.

Later that evening Harriet awoke from her sleep, she was so worried for her father and Kira that she sat up quickly to look out the window to see if she could see anything, in hopes that they would walk up the path at any minute, but she knew in her heart that this was unlikely.

She was about to give up but just as she was about to avert her eyes away from the window she noticed something at the edge of the forest. What was it? Harriet thought. It was a very faint glowing Light. But then it disappeared, Harriet was puzzled, was it her father's Light from his staff? Was it Kira's or someone's Lēoht, she couldn't tell. Harriet kept her eye on the forest like a tiger hunting its prey, so focussed she dare not blink.

A minute went by which seemed like an hour and then she saw it again, a pair of white glowing balls of Light just hovering slowly then disappearing. Harriet was both petrified and curious -as the last time she saw similar looking lights in the forest it was the eyes of the Darkness watching her- but she let curiosity get the better of her and crept quietly towards the door of the hut so as to not wake her Mother. However, when she glanced towards her mother's bed, she was shocked to find it empty. Has she not returned, or did she come back and leave again? Harriet wondered. With a feeling of dread Harriet put her robe, shoes and gloves on and picked her lantern up off the floor. She went outside and the giant lantern was ablaze as it was every evening. Harriet had to be quiet and quick to get out of the village unseen, as it was forbidden for anyone to leave the confines of the village at night.

She tiptoed around the back of the hut to get out of the direct Light, sticking close to the wall. She knew it was the most stupid thing she could do going out alone in the Dark so late. She looked back at her hut, wondering if this was a good idea or not, but something in her told her that this was important, she didn't know how, she just knew. So she cast Invīsibilis, turning invisible in seconds and walked down the hill to the forests entrance where the pilgrims had not long since passed through. When she reached the entrance to the forest she crouched and placed her lantern on the floor. The lantern was an exquisite looking artefact her mother had given to her; it was made from silver and had some engraved markings on it too, but Harriet did not know their meaning. It had three solid little legs that coiled up on themselves like springs to support it and a sturdy circular handle for Harriet to carry it from. The glass orb for the Light source was secured within the centre of the metal housing which was crafted so that it allowed for Light to be sent out in all directions. Harriet clasped her hands loosely around the glass orb and said "Lēoht" in a soft voice so as to not make any sound, instantly lighting up the lantern. She picked it up by its handle and carried on walking towards the edge of the forest.

As she grew closer she could see faint shapes among the Darkness -since Harriet could remember, she had been scared to go out in the Dark from seeing these ghostly beings lingering in the forest. They were only visible like this at night, in the daytime she could only just faintly see them -like little waves of heat rising from a scorching fire. Judging that no one else ever said anything or acknowledged that they existed in any way, she just assumed that she was the only person that could see them, so she kept it to herself as her own little secret.

These transparent, ghostly figures were all completely motionless, staring at her with big, black eyes, or were they holes for eyes, she could not tell. Harriet was so frightened to be this close to them that she got goose bumps all over her and did not want to go any closer, but the thought of her father and Kira and the others in danger drove her to push on. She cast Lēoht on her lantern again to intensify its brightness and the ghostly figures moved backwards into the Darkness of the forest, away from the Light. She had reached the barrier that protected the village. The barrier did not allow anyone through, it was as solid as rock. Harriet wondered if she could pass through it using her Invīsibilis, so she took one hand off of her lantern and held it up slowly, edging it towards the barrier. As her hand neared the solid Light it started to dissolve around it, she pulled her hand out and it sealed shut again.

"It worked," Harriet said aloud, before realising that she needs to be quiet.

She held onto her lantern with both hands again, closed her eyes and stepped through the barrier, opening them and looking back to see the barrier seal shut once more. As she got closer to the figures, she saw that they looked different to the humongous, Darkness monster she saw the previous evening. Something was friendly about these beings, whatever they were.

Harriet stepped into the forest. It was pitch black and the Light from her lantern was dimming, as if it was being suffocated by the Darkness. There was no sound of wildlife or insects in the forest, only the wind that was soaring past her ears and the crackling of trees. She was gazing around to see if the monster was anywhere near, but the only thing she saw aside from these glowing figures was the white balls of Light she saw from her window, floating among the trees just a few metres away. They were now like half moon and crescent moon shapes, growing and shrinking in size. Harriet held her lantern up in front of her to see where she was walking, wearily wading through the dense undergrowth of the forest, stepping through the big tree roots and weeds trying not to get entangled and trip over.

As she approached these strange floating Lights, her lantern lit up a cocoon like object hanging from the tree branch with crescent moon shaped lights at the bottom of it. Harriet lifted her lantern up closer to inspect it and gasped. It was a great big bat hanging from the tree, and it was nearly half her size. She put her hand up to her mouth screaming into her glove to soften the noise. Startled from what she saw she quickly stepped backwards and tripped over on the undergrowth, dropping her lantern to the side of her. The Light and sound of her shrieking and falling down startled the bat and woke it up, casting its huge, beady white eyes -much like the Darkness monster she saw- at Harriet and let go of the branch, twisting its body round to float in mid air, flapping its wings, bobbing up and down in the Darkness like a boat in the sea.

Harriet was now stiff with fear; she was sat huddled against an entanglement of roots with her knees pressed against her chest, one hand covering her mouth to dampen her screams and the other hand holding the lantern in front of her as a ward to scare off this ghastly bat. Harriet shut her eyes and cried a fearful scream into her glove as she could hear its wings pushing the air around her, wafting her hair, edging towards her slowly.

Still curled up on the floor, she could sense that the bat was right next to her. Then something happened which Harriet could never have imagined in her wildest dreams. The bat spoke.

"Hello... Child of Light."

Chapter 5 - The Shrine

Minutes had gone by and Harriet was still sat shaking in fear when the bat spoke to her again.

"Hello child," his voice was very old and croaky like an elderly man.

"Arrgghhhhh!" she screamed into her glove once more.

"Please. Do not be scared child, for I am here to aid you. My name is Cyril. There is no need for your introduction. I know who you are Harriet," Harriet stopped screaming and slowly looked up from behind her knees through squinting eyes.

"How... do you know my name?" she asked still quivering and scared stiff, ignoring the fact that a giant bat was talking to her.

"I know everything about you Harriet. I have been watching over you since you were born."

"You have been watching me? Why?" she asked him.

"Because you are the Light which will save us all from Darkness and I am here to watch over you. I am your Guardian."

"My... Guardian?" Harriet asked. She was now sat upright trying to untangle herself.

"Yes. Long ago... just before you were born, the Spirit of Light tasked me to watch over you until the time came when I must aid you."

Harriet was speechless for a moment, trying to take in what he was telling her. She had managed to get free of the undergrowth and was sat up on a great big tree root, holding her lantern on her lap. She looked up at Cyril, now less scared but more intrigued by him.

"Why me? Why am I so special for the Spirit of Light to assign me a Guardian, and to guard me from what? I do not understand."

"I cannot say any more Harriet. That is all I can tell you. The path is already laid out for you to follow, you just have to walk it," she had no idea what Cyril meant, she was more focussed on his eyes.

"Why are your eyes like that? They are like the eyes of the Darkness I saw."

"I am from a different place Harriet. I am a half-spirit. It allows me to travel between planes."

"Between planes, what do you mean?" she asked curiously.

"There are three planes Harriet; the Plane of Light, the Plane of Darkness and between them in the middle is this one, the Plane of the Living. These worlds existed simultaneously on top of each other as one. Well, that was until the Darkness broke free of its prison."

Harriet's mouth was hanging open in amazement.

"So these beings in the Forest, are they from another plane then?"

"That is correct Harriet. When the Darkness broke free, something disrupted the link that separated these planes and they are now aimlessly wandering between them. They seem to like it here in this plane though."

Harriet suddenly remembered her father, Kira and the others.

"Mr Cyril, do you know what happened to my father and the other villagers?"

"Yes I do Harriet, but it would be too difficult for me to explain, you will need to see for yourself."

"What do you mean see for myself?" she asked.

"If you follow this path we will reach the shrine. If you wish to know what happened then that is where we must go."

"To the shrine, but I am not allowed to go there."

"The time has come where you must child," Cyril flew over to the pathway. "Come child, let us go there and you will understand."

Harriet expected the worst, but she needed to know what happened to everyone.

"The Darkness. It will come for me now I am in the forest though."

"You have Invīsibilis Harriet, he cannot see you. Also he is not in this plane anymore, he has gone back to the Plane of Darkness where he came from. So you need not worry."

Harriet still felt like she was not safe out here and then realised she had been invisible the entire time Cyril was talking to her.

"You can see me?" she asked him.

"Yes child, I can see all of the planes and everything within them, spirits, Darkness and the Light."

Harriet was finding it hard to get her head around everything that was going on. Cyril was the most bizarre and incredible thing she had ever come across. She was not scared of him anymore, just extremely curious to know more about him.

"So how old are you Mr Cyril?" she asked him, not even considering if it was rude to ask him a question like that so directly.

"I am as old as time itself child," she held her lantern up to take a look at him properly and noticed that he had white hairs all over him and a fluffy white beard.

"You have a beard? Bats do not have beards do they?" she was puzzled and mildly amused at a bat with a fluffy beard.

"When you have lived as long as I have then yes child."

Harriet giggled under her breath. But Cyril heard her laugh and gave her a blank stare in response.

"So..." Harriet paused awkwardly, unsure if to ask him or not "The Spirit of Light... what is she like?"

"She is a lovely being and she is like a mother to me. But I have not seen her in a while now, she has gone missing," he looked saddened as he said this.

"She is missing?"

"Yes child. Not long after the Darkness broke free, she decided to head to the Plane of Darkness to confront him. But she never returned."

"Oh no, that explains why the Darkness is growing so strong then."

"Correct, without the Spirit of Light the Darkness will continue to grow in power."

"How can it be stopped?"

"That will all become apparent soon Harriet. We are nearly at the shrine."

Harriet continued along the muddy path still soft from the footsteps of the Pilgrims, with Cyril still floating by her side. She realised that she was now totally surrounded by these spirits which seemed to be following her even though she was invisible. The spirits were scared of her lanterns Light and from a distance Harriet imagined that they looked like hundreds of moths trying to get to a single bright Light, but all of them too scared to touch it.

"They are harmless Harriet. They are just curious about you is all."

Harriet said nothing in response, looking around at them all as she walked onwards through the forest. A faint sound began to reach her -like a wasp flying next to her ear. As they kept walking the sound grew louder and was now starting to cause a slight rumble in her head.

"What is that noise Mr Cyril?" she asked as she looked around to see if something was flying near her ears.

"Soon you shall see Harriet. Keep walking, it is just down this hill and across the swamp."

Once they reached the bottom of this steep hill, the swamp that Cyril mentioned came into view. It had a wooden bridge running across it that was used by the pilgrims to cross over, but it had been destroyed and almost completely swallowed up by the swamp.

"What happened to the bridge Mr Cyril?" Harriet asked him.

"I do not know. I imagine that the Spirit of Darkness caused this in order to stop the Sorcerers getting to the shrine."

Harriet was looking around the swamp to see any other way to cross over, but she couldn't see anything.

"What are we going to do now Mr Cyril, we cannot cross it."

"There is a way we can Harriet. But you will need to turn off your lantern."

"...What, turn it off. But we will be in total Darkness," she looked scared at the idea.

"Do not worry Harriet, I am with you, nothing bad will happen. You must trust me," Cyril assured her.

"O...OK Mr Cyril, I will trust you," Harriet felt scared and a tingle of fear raced up her spine.

"Averte," Harriet said, depleting her lantern of all its light. She could not even see Cyril or her own hands in front of her face it was so dark.

"Mr Cyril?" she called out, "Are you still there?"

"Yes child. Always."

"What are we to do now Mr Cyril?"

Cyril was now making whispering noises, they sounded like a muffled language but Harriet could not understand it. The space around them became illuminated by the spirits that were following them, walking straight past and sometimes through Harriet and Cyril, down into the swamp.

"What...what is happening Mr Cyril?" she could now faintly see him due to the Light the spirits gave off.

"I have asked the spirits to help us. Look at the swamp child,"

Harriet watched the spirits, they were walking into the swamp and holding their hands up above the marshy water to create a bridge of Light.

"Oh...wow. That is just magnificent, can we walk across them?"

"Yes child, only you can walk across, not just anyone is capable of this."

"Why only me?" she asked him, but he ignored the question, "Come now Harriet, time is of the essence."

Harriet followed Cyril down to the swamp edge, noticing that the mud was becoming mushier the closer she got. Standing on wood at the start of the bridge -the only part that was left standing- she looked out across the swamp. The bridge of Light made by the helping spirits gave off a radiating, ethereal glow that lit up the muddy marsh below where broken pieces of wood could be seen half sunken among the reeds and mud below.

"All you need to do is walk across Harriet. Do not be afraid."

Harriet did not even question Cyril and began to walk forwards to the edge of the wooden frame, when she was about to take her first step onto the spirits hands she hesitated.

"Will it hurt them Mr Cyril?"

"No child you will not," Cyril floated ahead of her, as if he was assuring her to move forward and take the step.

Harriet gently took the first step down on to the spirits hands. As she placed her foot down she realised that it was a solid platform and she was not actually standing on their hands.

"See Harriet, the Light is here to aid you."

"This is so strange, how did they make this bridge?" Harriet said walking at a slow pace and looking down at the spirits below. Some of the spirits were deeper than others and the ones that had their heads

144

above the swamp were watching her as she walked over them.

"The combined Light from their hands joins to form a solid form of Light, but only you have the power to walk over it, anyone else would fall right through into the swamp."

Harriet was not listening fully to Cyril as she was too busy looking at the Light that dispersed when her feet touched the Bridge, pulsing out a wave of Light like ripples from stepping in a puddle.

As they stepped onto the ground the other side of the swamp Harriet turned to look at the Bridge once more. The spirits had dispersed and the Bridge disappeared. Instead of the spirits following them as they were before, they only gathered together and stood at the edge of the swamp watching them, as if they did not want to go any further.

"Why are they not following us anymore Mr Cyril?" Harriet asked him.

"Because they are frightened of what is behind these trees."

"Frightened, but they are spirits. Why would they be frightened?"

"Because the Spirit of Darkness can still consume them and they wish to remain far away from the shrine. They only came this close to it because you needed their help."

Harriet wondered why she was so special that they would come to aid her even though it was dangerous for them.

"We are almost there Harriet, just a little further. You can Light your Lantern again now."

"Lēoht" Harriet said, now able to see Cyril properly again.

They continued walking into the forest with the swamp behind them, edging ever closer to the shrine. The buzzing noise Harriet heard before was now increasing in volume and a faint Light could be seen breaking through the opening in the trees ahead. As they reached this opening Harriet could partially see a structure of some sort on the other side. She walked through to see it in its full glory; an enormous monument towered high into the treetops with huge steps leading down from it, down on to a small grassy field. Trees looped around the field and around the back of the structure.

"That is the shrine child. We are here."

"I never imagined it to be *that* huge."

"It had to be that big to contain the Darkness within it," Harriet then realised the buzzing was coming from the shrine. She was not sure if it was the Darkness within the confines of the shrine or the Light surrounding it that was making the sound. But all the while it freaked her out.

All around the floor she saw pale objects. Curiously she walked over to them to see what they were. As she got close to one she shone her lantern on it and could not believe what she saw. It was a body. She looked around and saw that there was bodies scattered everywhere, in the trees, the Forest and all over the field in front of the shrine. These bodies were the villagers that had come on their pilgrimage to seal the Darkness away. She saw one of the villagers she recognised, it was Kira's father. The Light from the orb he was carrying had died out and his body was so pale it gave off a radiating white glow like the Moon.

"This is so awful. Are they dead?" she asked Cyril through teary eyes.

"Their spirit has been stolen by the Darkness," he replied.

"Stolen?"

"Yes. The Darkness seems to be stealing spirits to build his own power."

"Can they be saved Mr Cyril?" she said as she let the tears fall down her cheeks.

"I do not know Harriet. This has never happened before. That is why I need your help."

"But what can I do?" she asked him, not knowing how she could be of any assistance.

"The Spirit of Light has left part of herself in you. Do you not remember the events that took place in the forest a few days ago?"

"No Mr Cyril, I do not have any memory of it at all."

"I see..." he said rather puzzled.

Harriet then heard something rustle in the forest, just over the other side of the grassy field which was littered with these spiritless villagers. She was tiptoeing over the bodies, looking for any sign of Kira and her father, but she could not see either of them anywhere. A pale Light was glowing from behind a tree so she cautiously walked over to investigate.

"Be careful Harriet," Cyril begged her as she began to walk over to see what it was. She edged cautiously to the tree and peeked around it slowly, not knowing what was there. A figure slowly came into view and she saw that it was a person. She walked around to see who it was and was taken aback to realise that it was her father. He was sat huddled against the tree, wide eyed and looking absolutely petrified.

"Father!" Harriet cried. He slowly turned his head and looked up at her.

"Harriet? You came." His voice sounded weak and traumatised.

"Of course I did, I knew something was wrong and had to see for myself."

"Well done Harriet. Please help me up," Harriet bent down and pulled him up off the ground.

"We must be quick to act Harriet. You must go into the Darkness between the shrine."

"What. Are you crazy? How is that going to help, I will lose my spirit like the rest of these people."

"You will not. Only you can pass through into the Plane of Darkness. The Spirit of Light chose you Harriet. It is what you are destined to do."

She looked at the shrine and then down at the lifeless bodies, picturing herself suffering the same fate.

"I will die just like them. I cannot do that Father."

"YOU MUST!" he shouted. Harriet was stunned at his shouting and turned to Cyril for advice.

"What... what am I to do Mr Cyril?" hoping that he held the answer.

"He is correct Harriet. You have been chosen by the Spirit of Light for a reason."

"So... I have to go into the Plane of Darkness? Is there no other way?" She hoped that there was.

"It is the only option we have left Harriet. There *is* no other way. I think that is what the Spirit of Light wanted you to do when she gave you her powers."

"What if I do not go? What will happen to my home and these people?" she asked him.

"I fear that they will die and the world will be shrouded in Darkness like it almost was before."

"You must embrace the Darkness to find the Light," said Alucio.

"If that is what I must do then so be it. I do not want people to die because of me. Will you be coming with me Cyril?"

"Of course I will child. I am your guardian through all of this."

"Good. Then let us go, it seems there is no other alternative. Father please tell mother that I love her and I will see her soon."

"I will do little one, thank you," he gave her a hug and kissed her on the cheek. "Take care of my girl Cyril."

"I will do Sir, you have no need to worry, she is under my protection," he said as he glared at him, like he was checking him over for something. Harriet noticed but did not give it any thought.

"OK, let us get this over with," Harriet said.

Harriet turned to face this terrifying task ahead of her, gazing wearily at the shrine, marvelling at the huge archway containing the Darkness. The shrine was so vast in size and its height was tremendous and monstrous much like the beast it contained. The architecture looked gothic and incredibly ancient; a large stone triangular archway grew upwards from the ground to a massive spike that peaked high into the sky as if it pierced the clouds above. Down both sides of it, triangular extrusions stuck out to a point which supported 3 giant orbs on each side, with one on the top peak, housing a powerful Light created by the Elders which forced the Darkness into the space between the arches. But the Light was fading and now the seal was nearly at breaking point. In the middle of the huge arch was the Darkness; the corrupt spirit that once tried to sap all Light from the world. It looked like a cloud of smoke stuck between two panes of glass.

Harriet cautiously walked forward to climb its huge steps. Her full attention was on the Darkness between the huge pillars, eyes as wide as an owl, not blinking, not taking her gaze off it for even a second. She did not know what to expect. She had never seen the shrine until now as it was hidden down a hill, deep within the Forest, and out of sight from the village. Harriet was clasping her hands together holding her lantern, twiddling her thumb nails together anxiously. She glanced around at the bodies lying on the floor and was frightened this would happen to her too. She walked carefully through the field of bodies towards the shrine and climbed its steep steps, still focussed solely on the Darkness. The archway began to creak and shake the ground, the Darkness had been disturbed. Harriet stared terrified at the enormous arch which was now starting to rattle. Her eyes were fixed on it as the Darkness was beginning to break through -like snakes trying to escape a pool of water. The Darkness became angry, it was like an earthquake and she was at its core.

"Mr Cyril... I am so scared," she said as she was trembling all over.

"I am with you Harriet no matter what," he assured her.

"Thank you. Truly."

"No need to thank me Harriet, it is my honour to be your guardian. Now let us go forth and find the Spirit of Light. She needs us."

She knew that nothing good would come of this, but what choice did she have? she asked herself. Even her father told her this is what she needed to do, so maybe this would lead her towards the answer. Or maybe this was a false hope and a similar fate to those who lay around her awaits. As Harriet approached the shrine, streams of Darkness were lashing out in the air trying to latch on to her, but the Light from her lantern warded them off like a protective shield.

For a moment she stood there, motionless, staring at the lashing streams, as if all life around her had stopped, just watching at how the Darkness was trying so hard to grab onto her. She looked at Cyril who gave her a nod as if to say it is OK. She nodded back to him. Then courageously, in a dull, sad tone as if she had accepted her death Harriet said, "Averte," and the Light in her lantern went out.

She could sense the sinister intent of the Darkness. The once whipping streams now grew slowly towards her and she bravely accepted their touch. Darkness embraced Harriet and Cyril like a snake constricting its prey, clouding them in a cocoon of Darkness, unknowing of what was to come next. It lifted them high off the ground as if it was inspecting them, before it began pulling them into the void between the arches.

Just before passing through into the Darkness, Harriet caught a glimpse of her father who was now standing at the top of the steps, staring directly at her. His now bright white eyes shone vividly and an evil smile crossed over his face. The Darkness pulled them through, and as she sunk into the Dark abyss, she saw her own body, lifeless on the shrine floor.

To be continued...

6482127R00089

Printed in Great Britain
by Amazon.co.uk, Ltd.,
Marston Gate.